EX
LIBRIS

THE PAINTING

CHARIS COTTER

tundra

Tundra Books, an imprint of Penguin Random House Canada Young Readers,
a Penguin Random House Company

Library and Archives Canada Cataloguing in Publication

Cotter, Charis, author
The painting / Charis Cotter.

Issued in print and electronic formats.

ISBN 978-1-101-91887-6 (hardback).—ISBN 978-1-101-91888-3 (epub)

I. Title.

PS8605.O8846P35 2017   jC813'.6   C2016-906913-3
C2016-906914-1

Published simultaneously in the United States of America by Tundra Books
of Northern New York, an imprint of Penguin Random House Canada
Young Readers, a Penguin Random House Company

Library of Congress Control Number: 2016956781

Edited by Samantha Swenson
Designed by Terri Nimmo and Jennifer Griffiths
The text was set in Harriet Text.

Cover illustration © 2017 by Jensine Eckwall
Painting on page 278 reproduced with permission from the Squires family.

Printed and bound in the USA

www.penguinrandomhouse.ca

1   2   3   4   5   21   20   19   18   17

Penguin
Random House
tundra   TUNDRA BOOKS

For my mother, Evelyn Cotter, 1923–2013

PART ONE

THE CALL

"Take care of yourself!" screamed the White Queen, seizing Alice's hair with both her hands. "Something's going to happen!"

CLAIRE

I WAS COLD. I struggled up through a dream of long white corridors and breaking glass into my freezing bedroom, which
was filled with the white light of the full moon. An icy Atlantic
breeze inched its way through the gaps in the window frame
and slithered around my bed.

I jumped up, ran to the trunk in the corner and hauled out
a red woolen blanket. As I turned to get back in bed, the moon
pulled at me, and I wrapped the blanket around my shoulders
and sat down in the big stuffed armchair. The glowing disc of
the moon spilled light in a wide path across the water.

The beacon from the lighthouse flashed over the silver sea,
a steady rhythm, every five seconds. Like a heartbeat. Like a
drum.

"Annie," I whispered. "Where are you?"

ANNIE

T HE FIRST TIME I had the dream was the night of Mom's accident. The house was quiet. A stillness spread out from my parents' room.

I lay there for a long time, listening. The curtains were open and a full, silvery moon shone in the window, as bright as a streetlight. Its beam fell on the painting of a Newfoundland lighthouse opposite my bed. It looked different than it did in daylight, transformed by the moonlight into black and white, with sharper outlines and deeper shadows.

A white seabird with black-tipped wings swooped across the dark clouds—I blinked. For just a second I thought I had actually seen the bird moving across the painted surface. I sat up. As I watched, another bird leaped forward and dived into the silver ocean with a splash.

"Annie!" called a faraway voice. I scrambled out of bed.

"Annie!" called the voice again. There was something familiar about it, but it wasn't coming from downstairs, nor from my parents' bedroom down the hall. I turned and stared at the painting. I took a step toward it. Now I could see more details: patches of wildflowers by the side of the road leading to the lighthouse, a few sheep grazing on the hill, lights glowing behind the windows of the keeper's house.

Suddenly the blades of grass in the foreground trembled. A wave passed through the meadow grasses. Then another. I felt a gust of wind on my face, and a wild, unfamiliar smell filled the room. I could taste salt on my lips and I could hear the seabirds crying as they swooped across the sky.

"Annie!" cried the voice again. "Come!"

I took a step forward.

Then I was inside the painting, standing on the road to the lighthouse, with a surprised sheep raising its head to stare at me and the dark ocean stretching away as far as I could see.

———

I rubbed my eyes. It didn't help. The moonlit landscape was still there all around me, with the sharp Atlantic wind blowing my hair across my face. A sweet scent rose from the long grass as it rippled in the wind.

"Annie!" called the voice.

I took a step forward. Then another. The road was mostly sheep-cropped grass, cool under my bare feet, but every now and then I stepped on a sharp stone. The chill wind cut through my blue cotton pajamas.

Every so often I'd stumble into a puddle of water on the road, and the cold made me gasp. A few steps through squelchy mud and then I was on the grassy path again.

"Annie!" called the voice again, coming right from the lighthouse above me. I hurried up the road, the rocks digging into my feet, rounded the last corner and I was there.

The house loomed up, two stories high, with the dark-red lighthouse towering over it. It had two front doors. I knocked on the first one. The knock echoed through the house, but no one came. I knocked again. All I could hear was the ocean waves steadily beating at the rocks below. I knocked one more time. No answer. I pushed open the door and went in.

———

I was in a dark hallway. A staircase opposite the door led upstairs.

"Annie!" The voice was a whisper now, coming from the second floor.

Slowly I mounted the steps. My bare feet made no sound. A shaft of moonlight shone in through a small window at the top of the stairs, and I could just make out three closed doors to my left.

"Annie," came the whisper again, very faint now. It came from behind the first door. I turned the handle and opened it slowly.

A figure sat by the window, gazing out at the moon hanging over the ocean. It was a girl about my age, with light-brown hair falling over her shoulders. She was wrapped in a red woolen blanket.

"Hello?" I said.

The girl screamed and jumped straight up in the air. She came down scrambling and huddled against the window frame, still clutching her red blanket and staring at me with eyes as round as the moon behind her.

"Sorry," I said, catching my breath. Her scream had jolted me. "But I thought I heard you calling me."

"Annie?" the girl croaked. "Annie, is that you?"

"I'm Annie, but who are you?"

She took a faltering step toward me. "You've changed. You're older."

"I . . . uh . . . older than what?" I said. My head was starting to spin.

"Older than when I last saw you. You were only four. But don't you recognize me? I'm Claire, your big sister Claire."

I shook my head. "There must be some mistake. I don't have a sister."

She edged a little closer, studying my face and frowning. "You're definitely Annie, but I don't know why you look so much older now."

Before I could answer, a door slammed and I heard quick footsteps in the hall. The girl leaped toward me and started pushing me toward the bed.

"It's Mom! Hide!"

Without thinking, I scrambled under the bed and lay holding my breath as Claire bounced into the bed and the bedroom door slammed open.

"Claire, what's wrong? I heard you scream." The woman had a husky voice and she sounded sleepy.

"I don't know," mumbled Claire. "I guess I had a bad dream."

The woman sat down on the bed with a thump and I got a good whack on the head. I just managed not to yell out.

"What am I going to do with you, Claire?" said the woman, heaving a big sigh. "I thought you were getting past this."

"Mmmmphhh."

Silence.

"Are you okay?" said the woman finally.

"Just let me go back to sleep," said Claire. Silence.

A corner of the bedspread was hanging down in front of me. The moon lit up the edge of it. The blue-and-white pattern looked very familiar. I reached out and felt the thick circles of quilted material. I had felt those interlocking circles before. Many times. It was the quilt from my bed, the one I had been sleeping under that very night when I heard the voice calling me. My quilt.

———

It happened in the blink of an eye—one minute I was lying under Claire's dusty bed, my fingers tracing the outlines of circles on the quilt, and the next I was sitting on my bed, the quilt soft under my hand, staring at the painting of the lighthouse. It looked like it had always looked—a quiet seascape with the red tower of a lighthouse stark against the sky. No birds swooping, no sheep raising their heads to look at me. I lay back and pulled the quilt up to my chin and closed my eyes. A dream. It was all a dream.

CLAIRE

I T MUST HAVE been a dream. That's what I told myself the next morning as I sat at the breakfast table stirring brown sugar into my corn flakes. I must have fallen asleep in the chair and dreamed that Annie came back.

Annie. I'd sat at that window and called her so many times. Hoping she would come back to me. I didn't care if she was a ghost. I just wanted to see her again.

After she died I saw her all the time. I didn't have to call. Every time I opened my closet she'd be there. I'd look up from my desk at school to see her standing beside me. Or she'd be sitting in her usual place at the breakfast table. Or on the sidewalk looking up at the house. Always silent. Always staring at me with unblinking eyes. I was scared to go to the bathroom at night, afraid she would be behind the shower curtain.

Finally one day while I was watching TV with Nan, Annie appeared beside me on the couch and I lost it. I jumped up and started screaming at her to go away.

My mom took me to a psychiatrist. He said I was still grieving for my dead sister and then asked me to sit outside while he talked to my mom. The door wasn't quite shut and I could hear them.

"Does she blame herself for her sister's death?" asked the doctor.

"I don't know," said my mother. "It was an accident."

"You must do everything you can to reassure her," said the doctor.

"I've been planning to move out of town," said my mother. "For a while now. Maybe a new environment will help."

"Maybe," said the doctor.

The next week we moved away from St. John's to Crooked Head Lighthouse, in the middle of nowhere, and Annie never came back. No matter how many times I called.

Sometimes I think I can't go on living with my heart broken in two like this. It's supposed to get better in time, that's what people say. That you stop missing the dead person every minute of every day. But after four years, I still keep hoping she'll come back to me.

She was too little to die, too little to go wherever the spirits of the dead go. She still needs me. I still need her. I'm lonely.

Last night it felt so real. Not like a dream at all.

I glanced at the old clock on the mantel. Oops. Ten past eight. There were only two weeks left before the holidays, but the nuns teachers were strict. If I was late, I had to stay in for recess.

I slapped a peanut butter and jelly sandwich together, wrapped it up in wax paper, grabbed an apple and stuffed it all into my schoolbag. Took my raincoat off the peg in the hall and ran out the front door.

Mom never got up before ten. Or later. She's a night owl. She trained me when I was seven to get up and make my own breakfast and lunch for school, and I'd been doing it ever since. Annie used to wake me up early and we'd lie in bed talking for a while, then I'd get up and make her breakfast.

A brisk wind blew off the ocean, ruffling my hair. It was clear, and I could see the headlands climbing into the distance away north and the indigo sea stretching on forever to the east. I set my face to the west and hurried down the path that led to the village. It was a two-mile walk, and I'd have to run part of the way or be late.

ANNIE

THE NEWFOUNDLAND PAINTING had been hanging on the wall opposite my bed for about eight months. Before that it had stood behind an old wooden trunk in the attic, wrapped in the blue-and-white quilt, for who knows how long.

I found it one rainy day when I was looking for my picture books. Once I finally learned how to read at the end of grade two, my mother took all my picture books away and stashed them in the attic. "You're too old for these now, Annie," she'd said. I missed them. To me, the pictures of a story were what held my attention. They said so much more than the words. Every once in a while I go up in the attic and look at my books by the

13

dim light from the bare bulb overhead, turning the pages slowly.

I hadn't been to the attic for a while, and my mother must have rearranged things, because the cardboard box with my books in it wasn't where it used to be. As I poked around among the piles of old furniture and boxes, I came across a big wooden trunk that I'd never noticed before. Behind it I could see a lumpy shape, wrapped in a blue-and-white quilt.

I liked what I could see of the circles sewn into the quilt. I reached out to touch it and felt a hard frame beneath it. I hauled the whole thing, quilt and all, out into the middle of the attic, where the overhead bulb cast its yellow ring of light.

The quilt was a lovely thing: large interlocking circles made of various shades of small blue squares, from light turquoise to deep indigo, set against a white background. It was a bit faded, but the shades of blue still held some vibrancy, slipping from light to dark and then back to light again, the colors leading my eyes from one circle to another until I got lost in it. I gave my head a shake and then let the quilt fall away to see what lay beneath.

It was a painting, set in a heavy wooden frame carved into thick swirls. A grassy foreground, a road leading through rocky hills to a lighthouse, and a vast ocean beyond. Something about it seemed familiar. I'd never been to the ocean. Maybe a photograph I'd seen somewhere? Or even a picture in one of my old picture books? I brought the quilt down to my bed and leaned the painting against my wall.

I sat on the bed, feeling the thick circles of cloth under my fingers, and looked at the painting.

In the better light I could see some sheep grazing at the base of one of the hills and white seabirds with black wingtips flying against the gray sky. A falling-down rail fence climbed halfway up a hill.

When my mother got home from work that night and stuck her head in my room, I was lying on the quilt with my sketch-book and colored pencils, drawing the lighthouse. She stood there for a minute with her mouth hanging open.

I smiled at her.

She closed her mouth and came into the room, reaching out her hand to touch the quilt.

"What are you doing with this, Annie?" she asked. Then she saw what I was sketching and turned and saw the painting.

"Oh," she said and sat down suddenly on the bed.

"I found it in the attic," I said. I held out my sketch to her. She glanced at it. It wasn't bad: the white-and-blue house with the tall red lighthouse rising above the roof. I liked the four-square shape of the house, with its two front doors and the windows lined up in rows.

She took my sketchbook and flipped back the pages. I'd been drawing studies from the painting for a couple of hours: the curve of the road, a couple of sheep, the lighthouse against the stormy sky, the grasses in the foreground. She stopped at a study of the grasses and reached out her finger to touch one of the golden, nodding stalks. She seemed to have forgotten me. She looked like she was thinking of something far away in time and space.

"Where is this?" I asked. She closed the sketchbook.

"It's Newfoundland, Annie. I've told you about Newfoundland."

"You said it was cold and gray and raining all the time."

"Most of the time," she said, and stood up, smoothing her skirt and turning her back to the painting. "I should have got rid of that picture years ago. I don't see why you like it so much. It's just an old, rocky field."

It was so much more than just a rocky field, but I knew from experience that Mom and I seldom saw things the same way.

CLAIRE

MY MOM AND I never see things the same way. She's an artist. I'm not. Whenever we walk the path to Crooked Head together, she talks about this view and that view, and how she wants to paint those trees and that broken-down fence. But all I see is the lonely road winding through scrubby trees and climbing along the long ridge of land that joins up with the mainland over a skinny little causeway that floods whenever the seas are high. I see the ocean spreading out on both sides forever and the little houses along the shore that are too far away to be neighbors. I'd trade it all in a minute for Gower Street in St. John's, with its tall houses tucked together in rows and firm pavement underfoot.

My mother had wanted to move out of St. John's for a long time. She was always piling Annie and me into the car and driving out to Crooked Head to paint. I would keep Annie busy playing while Mom worked at her easel, humming and frowning. She didn't like to be interrupted. Then on the way back to town, with Annie falling asleep against my shoulder in the back seat, Mom would talk on and on, almost to herself, about how she needed to be closer to nature for her art. And how she wanted to live at Crooked Head Lighthouse.

My Nan's family were lighthouse keepers at that lighthouse for about a hundred years, and my great-granddad, Poppy Morrow, was the last keeper there. Mom used to stay there summers when she was growing up, and she loved it more than anywhere on earth. That's what she told us, again and again, on those long rides home in the dark.

Crooked Head Lighthouse is about two hours south of St. John's. The lighthouse and the town were named for the huge twisted headland that looms over the bay. But in Newfoundland, *crooked* also means bad-tempered, and that's how I see this place. Gloomy and cranky and out of sorts. Like me.

I didn't always hate it. Nan used to come along sometimes on my mother's painting expeditions and take Annie and me to the lighthouse for picnics. No one had lived there since the light was automated a few years before, and Annie and I would run all over the house, exploring. There were still some sticks of furniture left behind, a few old dishes, some books. We would sit on an orange plaid car blanket, high above the water with our sandwiches, watching the whales jump and the gannets soar over the snappy whitecaps, and Nan would tell us stories about growing up at the lighthouse.

Summer picnics at the lighthouse were one thing. Living there all year round was another thing altogether. I later found out that my mother had been working on moving there for more than a year. She was determined, and she wangled her way through several government departments until she finally got permission to rent the lighthouse keeper's house at Crooked Head.

Annie died in June. Mom and I moved into the lighthouse in September. I left everything familiar behind in St. John's—our house, my school, my friends, Nan. And Annie.

ANNIE

T HE MORE I SAW of the painting, the more I admired the artist—the brushwork and colors were brilliantly done. But I think it was the gloomy, haunting mood that got under my skin. I asked Mom if we could go to Newfoundland someday, but she got mad and said she never wanted to set foot in that godforsaken place again.

I had to make do with looking at the painting every day, trying to imagine what it was like to live in that stormy, barren landscape. I did countless studies in my sketchbook. That must be why I dreamed about it. The painting got inside my head. Then I got inside the painting. It had all seemed so real.

Nothing seemed real when I woke up the day after my mother's accident. The house still had that strange, too-quiet feeling that made me feel as if the whole world was holding its breath. It was a big effort just to sit up, and I felt a tightness in my chest, like a weight was pressing on it. I slowly made my way down to the kitchen, feeling like I was moving through thick mud.

Dad was sitting at the table drinking coffee and stirring a bowl of milk and corn flakes. It was all mushy, as if he'd been stirring it for a long time.

He looked up at me.

"There's been no change," he said.

I sat down opposite my father, gazing at the sodden corn flakes in his bowl. They had an interesting texture—a lumpy orange swirled in white.

"Annie," said Dad sharply. I looked up. "You should eat."

I dragged myself to a standing position again and went to the counter to make some toast. When it popped out of the toaster, I put peanut butter and marmalade on it and sat down again. This was my favorite breakfast, but today it looked like something alien. I couldn't imagine eating it.

Dad poured me some juice. Then there was a commotion at the front door and Magda blew in.

Magda used to be my nanny, but then when I started school, she became our housekeeper instead. She comes by our place in the afternoons, doing laundry and housework and making me supper when Mom and Dad aren't home. She's Irish and worked in a hotel in Dublin until she got sick of it and immigrated to Canada. She tells me stories about all the rich people who stayed in the hotel and the strange things they did.

"Here I am," she said, plopping down her purse on the counter and reaching for the apron hanging on the back of the door. "The streetcar took forever. Would you believe it, the driver got off at Queen and Leslie to go get himself a coffee and left us all sitting there like a bunch of silly sheep, and a line of cars piling up behind us beeping and carrying on. Shall I make some muffins now, Annie? How about peanut butter and chocolate chip?"

She started hauling flour and baking soda and muffin tins out of cupboards.

"I don't know," I said. I felt like everything was off-kilter. "How come you're here in the morning, Magda?" I asked.

"I asked her to come," said Dad, pushing himself away from the table and standing up. "I don't think you should go to school today, and I have to go and see your mother."

"Can I come?" I asked.

He and Magda exchanged looks.

"Not yet," he said.

"Why not?"

They exchanged looks again. I didn't like that. How bad was she? Covered in bandages?

Blood? But they would have cleaned that up by now.

"Maybe you can come in a day or two. Once she's stabilized."

I had an image of Mom lying in a hospital bed, swinging through the air, back and forth, like a pendulum. Once it stopped, she would be stabilized. Then I could go.

CLAIRE

THE CROOKED HEAD LIGHTHOUSE stood alone on the edge of the Atlantic Ocean, nearly completely surrounded by water. Its only connection to the shore was that two-mile strip of land with a rough road that was impassable when it froze over in the winter or flooded in the spring. When we moved in, the keeper's house had been abandoned for a long time. Some of the windows were broken and the roof leaked.

Mom hired a man from the village to come and help her replace the windows and patch the roof. He was a large man named Ed, with a mustache and a big, friendly smile. He had a wife and three small children at home, and he couldn't understand what my mother was doing out there in that woebegone house with no man. He told her that at least once a week. My mother would laugh, but after he left she'd shake her head and say, "Newfoundland men are the most hidebound chauvinists in the world." When I asked her what a chauvinist was, she said it was a man who thought men were better than women, and that no woman was complete without a husband.

"Which is nonsense," she said. "Ed and his pals don't know what to think of a woman like me."

My mother liked to do things for herself. She got Ed to teach her how to frame up a window, shingle a roof and tape drywall. He brought in loads of firewood in his truck, and Mom taught me how to stack it in the porch. She made me haul heavy buckets of water from the well down the hill every day and pour it into the water barrel in the porch.

In those early days, we had no electricity and no indoor plumbing. We used candles and kerosene lamps and there was a makeshift toilet (a wooden box with a toilet seat and a pail underneath) in a cold little closet off the hall and a smelly outhouse round the back. Yuck. That's all I can say about that. Yuck.

I missed St. John's. My bedroom. My friends. The toilet.

ANNIE

M Y DREAM OF THE lighthouse stayed with me all that strange, silent day. Magda bustled around in the kitchen, baking the muffins and a chocolate cake and tuna casserole for supper—all my favorite foods. She'd check on me every once in a while, offer me food, talk my ears off for a few minutes, and then leave me alone again. I left my door open so I could hear the reassuring sound of her rattling dishes and muttering to herself, but it was just a tiny ripple in the growing silence of the house.

I went into my parents' bedroom. I opened the closet, ran my hands over Mom's skirts and jackets, her silky blouses. Looked at the neat row of shoes on the floor. Buried my head in her blue sweater, hanging on a hook on the door of her closet. It smelled like her.

Dad phoned a couple of times and talked to Magda, then me. No change.

And still the dream was there, hovering. The lighthouse. The moonlight on the ocean. Claire.

After lunch I sat on the bed, staring at the painting. The artist had signed her name in the bottom left-hand corner of the painting: Maisie King. Who was she? Why did Mom have her painting?

I could almost hear the silence in the house, the walls pressing in around me. I had that same heavy feeling in my chest that I'd felt when I woke up. It was a hot day, and all the windows were open, but there wasn't a breath of wind.

Suddenly I couldn't bear it anymore. I was halfway down the front steps when Magda caught up with me.

"Where are you off to?" she called.

"Library," I threw over my shoulder, and fled.

CLAIRE

C ROOKED HEAD IS haunted. I know it.

We moved into the lighthouse in September, just in time for the fall storms. One tropical storm after another made its way north and hurled itself at Crooked Head Lighthouse. The wind howled and roared around the house, which shook and rattled as if it was going to pick up and fly away over the Atlantic Ocean, like Dorothy's house in *The Wizard of Oz*.

We had two daybeds in the kitchen, one against each wall, where we slept, warm and dry. I would lie awake for hours, listening to the wind. It never screeched that way in St. John's. Sometimes it sounded like a human voice, rising and falling, shrieking, sobbing.

I made the mistake of talking to Ed about the wind one day when he was fixing holes in the walls of the room upstairs that was going to be my bedroom. He told me about the Old Hollies— the ghosts of all the people who had died in shipwrecks along this stretch of coast, before the lighthouse was built.

"You can still hear them screaming in the wind, begging for help," he said, shaking his head. "A terrible thing, a shipwreck. All those lives lost."

That night I was awake longer than ever, shivering in my bed while the wind moaned. I was convinced that a horde of shipwrecked ghosts was flying around the house, trying to get in. When I finally fell asleep, I dreamed that Annie was among them, calling my name, pleading with me to open the door. I woke up screaming her name.

My mother was not impressed when she found out what Ed had been telling me.

"There's no such thing as ghosts, Claire," she said. "Annie's gone. The wind is just the wind and Ed is a superstitious Neanderthal."

Mom told him not to tell me any more ghost stories, but he just laughed and winked at me.

It's not just Ed. My very first week at school, Mary Tizzard and Joan Crocker cornered me at recess and told me that Crooked Head Lighthouse was haunted by Isaac Morrow, an old man with scraggly white hair and no teeth, my great-great-great-grandfather, who died out there years ago. They said he sat on people's feet in the middle of the night. I tried not to look scared, but I don't think it worked because after that they came up with ghost stories nearly every week about ghosts that lurked all along my lonely route home: in the little woods where the road dipped out of sight, along the stony beach, on Pebble Island out in the bay.

From then on I walked the gauntlet of fear on the way to and from school. I kept my eyes peeled for phantom dogs running along the beach and skeletons clattering over the rocks by the causeway. I was continuously glancing over my shoulder, convinced that I was being followed by shadowy figures floating along the path behind me.

It was all very well for my mother to say there was no such thing as ghosts, but if that were true, I'd never see Annie again. So I believed all the ghost stories people told me and just prayed that I wouldn't encounter any ghosts.

Except for Annie.

ANNIE

OUR LOCAL LIBRARY is one of my favorite places, and it's just three blocks away from our house, so I go there a lot. It is about a hundred years old; it stands at the edge of a park and has a big table set in front of a soaring window that reaches up two stories and looks out onto the park.

I went to the shelves where the art books were and combed through them quickly. I found one called *Newfoundland Artists* and carried it over to the table by the window.

She was right there, in the index, under *K*. Pages 250 to 262. I flipped through the book, trying hard not to be distracted by the amazing paintings along the way. Ships, whales, endless seascapes, cliffs, jellybean-colored houses up a hill. Was this the cold and rainy Newfoundland Mom couldn't wait to get away from?

The very first painting under Maisie King was the one that hung on my bedroom wall. *Road to Crooked Head Lighthouse* was printed underneath it. On the opposite page was some text and a photograph of the artist. She had curly white hair clustered around her face, blue eyes, a big mouth and a straight nose.

As I gazed at her, her eyes seemed to sparkle and her mouth to twitch, as if she was about to burst out laughing. I closed my eyes for a moment, then looked again. She hadn't moved. I turned the page.

The painting on the next page was of the lighthouse again, but from the other side, as if the artist was in a boat just off the rocks, looking up at it. The lighthouse towered overhead, with the keeper's house behind it. Huge waves smashed against the rocks, and the sky roiled with dark-blue and black clouds. A jagged fork of lightning tore through the clouds to strike the glowing capsule of light at the top of the lighthouse.

As I looked at the painting, I began to feel a little sick, as if I was out in those tossing waves, rolling up and down in the swell. I put both hands on the edge of the book to steady myself and looked up. The library was quiet: business as usual. Mrs. Silver, an old lady who lived down the street from us, was nodding over a book at the far end of the table. She looked half asleep. The park outside the windows was green, and a couple of mothers stood chatting on the path, their babies snoozing in their strollers. Everything was normal and peaceful.

I looked back at the painting and the world tilted.

I felt like I was falling and my stomach heaved and I could hear a roaring of wind and a crash of thunder, and then I pitched forward, smashing my knees on a rock. A cold splash of water struck my back and I scrambled up the rocks, the waves nipping at my heels, rain pouring out of the sky, thunder and lightning crashing all around me. Above me the lighthouse light blinked steadily on and off.

Suddenly light and sound exploded together: a jagged spear of lightning hit the lighthouse, accompanied by a loud smack of thunder. Then, just as quickly, light and sound were sucked into darkness. The air crackled with electricity and I heard screaming in the wind. The light in the tower flashed on for a few seconds, illuminating the wet rocks and the dark, tumbling clouds, and then it blinked out. A few seconds later it burst into light again, then out, again and again. Like a slow heartbeat, sure and steady in the midst of all the chaos.

CLAIRE

THE DAY AFTER I had the dream that Annie came back, I walked home from school thinking about her, wondering if it really was her ghost or just a dream. Dark clouds were massing all along the southern horizon. There was going to be a storm.

I was going to an empty house—Mom was visiting Marjory,

an artist friend of hers, an hour's drive away in Blackberry Bight, and I'd be on my own for supper. That was fine with me. I liked having the place to myself.

I heated up a leftover hamburger and fried some potatoes, then settled to eat at the kitchen table with my latest ghost book (*The Eternal Shadow* by Philomena Faraday) propped up against the fruit bowl. Ever since Mary and Joan tried to scare the wits out of me, I'd been obsessed by the supernatural. I read all the ghost stories I could get my hands on.

A loud crash from upstairs roused me and I looked around, startled. It was very dark outside. The wind had picked up to an intense level of wailing and screeching. I caught my breath. The Old Hollies. Ed told me they always came just before a big storm when some disaster was about to happen. I shivered.

Then I told myself firmly in my mother's voice that it was only the wind and ran upstairs to my room, where the crash had been. A gust of wind had knocked over the floor lamp beside my chair and broken it, and the curtains were streaming into the room, whipped by the furious wind. I slammed the window shut just as the rain came down, torrents of it, as if someone had dumped a giant bucket over the house.

I went room to room, closing windows. Then I returned to the kitchen. It was darker than ever. I tried the light switch by the door, but there was no power. I found a candlestick on the dresser and fumbled in a drawer for matches. Soon a pale, flickering light filled the room. I carried the candle over to the wall and held it up so I could see the face of the clock. Six o'clock. Mom wouldn't be home for hours.

Just as I was turning away from the clock, the room exploded in a crash of noise and white light. The house shook under my feet and the front door slammed open in a gust of wind. I dropped the candle.

It fell right into the open wood box where we kept splits of wood and newspaper for starting the fire. The wind from the front door swept down through the hall into the kitchen and the paper went up in flames with a swoosh.

The fire crackled and leaped high into the air. The noise of the storm thundered into the house through the open door, and I heard voices screaming for help. I stood rooted to the spot, with the heat of the fire on my face and the Old Hollies howling all around me.

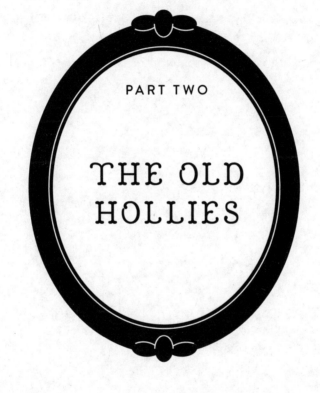

PART TWO

THE OLD
HOLLIES

I wonder if I've been changed in the night. Let me think: was I the same when I got up this morning? I almost think I can remember feeling a little different. But if I'm not the same, the next question is Who in the world am I? Ah, that's the great puzzle!

Alice, ALICE'S ADVENTURES IN WONDERLAND

ANNIE

THE BLINKING LIGHT lit my way for a few seconds and then plunged the night into darkness again. I tried to keep my balance and focus on where the rocks were as the light flashed on and off. I was completely soaked and I felt something warm and wet running down my shins: blood from where I'd bashed my knees. But I managed to scramble up the rocks on all fours and soon I came to a steep path. I half-ran, half-crawled up the slope and finally came out beside the lighthouse, gasping for breath.

In the striping light from the tower I could see a cloud of smoke billowing out from behind the house.

"Help! Help!" called the voices on the wind. I tore around the house to the front door and stumbled in, coughing. Through the smoke, I could make out the figure of a girl, outlined against a blaze of flames. The beacon from the lighthouse filled the room with bright light, illuminating her terrified face for a moment, and then blinked out.

It was Claire. She stood frozen, gaping at me.

The flames licked at the wall beside her. I lunged forward, grabbed her by the arm and pulled her away from the fire.

"Water!" I yelled above the roar of the storm. "We need water!"

CLAIRE

SHE WAS RIGHT there, in the kitchen, holding me by the arm and yelling at me about water. Annie.

I shook myself like a dog coming up out of a pond.

"Water!" yelled Annie again. "We need water!"

I pulled her toward the corner where two buckets stood on a table. We each grabbed one and dumped them over the flames.

"We need more!" she bawled in my ear. I turned and stumbled out the door through the drenching rain to the rain barrel at the corner of the house. The wind pulled at my clothes and hair, but Annie was right behind me and I pushed the thoughts of the Old Hollies out of my mind. The thunder was rumbling northward and the lightning crackled out over the ocean. We dipped our buckets into the rain barrel and ran back inside to try to douse the sputtering flames.

It took four trips to put out the fire. We stood panting in the dark kitchen, the floor slick with water under our feet, the light from the lighthouse glancing off our faces. One minute I could see her and the next minute the darkness swallowed her up.

"Annie," I said, reaching out and grabbing her hand so she wouldn't disappear completely again. "You saved my life."

ANNIE

I STARED AT HER. I had that tilting feeling again, only this time it wasn't the sea that was pitching and tossing, it was me—I felt like I was toppling over a cliff, held upright only by the steady pull of her bright eyes. I knew her. I felt that deep inside I knew her, but I didn't know from where. Her features were small, and she had a pinched look, like someone who was hungry all the time.

"If you hadn't come, I would have burned to death," she said, holding tight to my hand. "You saved my life, Annie!"

The light from the lighthouse flashed on and off. One minute she was there, her eyes shining brightly at me, and the next she was engulfed in darkness.

I pulled away. "I'm not . . . I just . . . I just heard you screaming for help and came in."

She shook her head. "That wasn't me screaming! It was the Old Hollies."

"Who are the Old Hollies?" I asked. "And why were they screaming? And where are they now?"

"Hang on a minute," said Claire. "I can't see you properly." She turned to the dresser and fumbled in a drawer. I heard the sound of a match striking as she lit a candle.

It made a golden bubble of light, with Claire in the middle, beaming at me.

"Annie," she said, "I'm so happy you've come back." She took a step closer and held the candle up so I was enfolded in the golden bubble too. She looked intently at my face, as if she was committing it to memory.

"You're different," she murmured. "I mean, I can see that you're Annie, but your face has changed."

That feeling of familiarity swept over me but I pushed it away. "I don't know you," I said. "You're mistaking me for someone else."

She shook her head. "No, I'm not. You're my sister Annie. I'd know you anywhere."

"I don't have a sister," I said. "I'm an only child. And anyway, this is just a dream."

"That's what I thought, last night. But I'm not dreaming now. You're my sister Annie who died four years ago."

CLAIRE

ANNIE LOOKED REALLY scared and started swaying like she was going to fall over. I grabbed her and steered her toward a chair. She sat down with a thump. Then I got her a glass of water.

She sipped it slowly, looking at me like I was the ghost.

"I'm not your sister," she said. "My name is Annie Jarvis. I live in Toronto. I've been having strange dreams ever since my mom went into the hospital. This is one of them."

I sat down opposite her. "Mom's not in the hospital. She's gone to Blackberry Bight to visit Marjory. She'll be back later tonight."

"You mean you're all alone out here? In the middle of the night? In a thunderstorm?"

I shrugged. "It's not the middle of the night. It's only just after six o'clock. I would have been fine except for the fire."

Just at that moment a long, eerie wail filled the air. The house shook and rattled in a sudden fierce gust of wind. Annie grabbed my arm, her eyes big.

"What is that?" she whispered. I could feel her shaking.

"Just the wind," I said, patting her hand. "Don't worry, Annie."

"But it sounds like people screaming! That's what I heard before. People calling for help."

I listened. The howling of the wind rose and fell. It went screeching around the house, then died away again.

"It's the Old Hollies," I whispered. "I never heard them so clearly before."

"What are they?" asked Annie.

"Ed says they're the spirits of all the shipwreck victims that died along this part of the coast."

"Who's . . . who's Ed?" stuttered Annie.

With a few more earsplitting screeches, the voices moved away. I could hear them racing along the cliffs and out to sea.

"Ed's our handyman. He has the best ghost stories." I patted her hand again. "It's okay, Annie, they're gone now. Ed says they come just before something terrible is going to happen, like a big storm, or a death in the family."

Annie's face crumpled.

"Oh no," she said, and began to cry.

ANNIE

"A NNIE!" CLAIRE JUMPED UP and put her arms around me. "Don't cry, sweetheart! It's okay."

I couldn't stop. Great gulping sobs came surging up out of me. I felt like I wanted to throw my head back and wail like the Old Hollies. Everything I had been holding in ever since we got the phone call about Mom came bubbling up and I couldn't bear it.

Claire kept patting my back and murmuring, "It's okay, Annie, it's okay, it will be all right," over and over again. Finally the tears subsided. Claire smelled like lavender soap. She was warm and kind and familiar. Who was she? I almost had it—but it slipped away.

"Hey," she said, pulling back and looking at me. "Better now?" She smiled gently. "This reminds me of how you used to cry when you hurt yourself when you were little. I could always make it better, couldn't I?"

I shook my head. "No. No. You don't understand. I'm not your sister. I'm really not your sister."

Claire shook her head. "You've forgotten, that's all. It happens. Ed told me sometimes ghosts wander for years, not knowing who they are or where they belong. That's why you're crying, because you're lost and you can't remember."

"No, I was crying because my mother is really sick and she's in the hospital, and when you said the Old Hollies were . . . were . . ." The tears were coming again and I tried to shake them off. "My mother might be dying. I'm so scared she's dying, and I thought maybe the Old Hollies were warning me—" I began to cry again.

"I don't understand," said Claire. "I've been calling you for so long, trying to get you back. And now you've finally come, but you're different and—"

"I heard you calling," I interrupted. "The other night. I was in my bedroom, right after I heard about Mom. I was sitting on the bed looking at the lighthouse painting—"

Claire went on talking as if she hadn't heard me. "I've missed you so much, Annie. I can't even tell you. It's so awful here and Mom's worse than ever. She hardly talks to me, just paints all the time. And I've got no friends because everyone thinks I'm a stuck-up townie, and all I want to do is go back to St. John's, but Mom says no, and I hate it here and—and—"

She grabbed my hand again and leaned toward me.

"I didn't mean it when I told you to go away before, I was just upset. Ever since then I've wanted you to come back. I miss you so much."

Her eyes were filling with tears, and for some reason I couldn't stand to see her cry. It hurt me, like something sharp was stuck inside my chest. I took a deep breath. It still hurt.

Claire wiped her eyes with the sleeve of her sweater. I cleared my throat.

"Umm . . . You've seen your sister's ghost before? You told her to go away?"

"Yes," she said, with a little frown. "Of course. Come on, Annie! You remember. Right after you died, you kept appearing everywhere, just staring at me, and I finally couldn't take it anymore and told you to go away. But then we moved here and you never came back. I'm sorry, Annie. I never should have told you to go away."

"How did it . . . how did she die? Your little sister."

"Don't you remember? You saw a neighbor's dog, that little black Scottie, Sammy, across the street, and you broke away from me and ran straight across the street and a car—a car—" She gulped and couldn't go on.

"How awful," I whispered. I reached out and took her hand. "I'm so sorry."

"It . . . it was horrible. I still have nightmares about it. Why did you have to run, Annie? Why did you always have to run?"

CLAIRE

S ITTING THERE, WITH Annie's hand in mine, looking into her eyes, it all came back to me in a rush. The way she was bouncing down the street beside me that day, and then when Sammy barked how she tore away from me, straight for Sammy across the street, and how I lunged after her and the car that was suddenly there and the squeal of brakes and the thump. That awful thump. I stopped just short of the car and stood there panting. I didn't want to go around and see what had made that thump. I knew it was Annie.

Grown-ups appeared from nowhere, a whole crowd of them, running and shouting, and somebody screamed and started to cry, and I just stood there, frozen. Then a neighbor took ahold of me and that's when I wanted to see Annie, and I struggled and cried and tried to go back, but the neighbor hauled me away.

So I didn't see her again. I wouldn't look at the funeral. I couldn't.

And now here she was, come back to me. Her hand was warm in mine. I squeezed it.

"Don't leave me again, Annie," I whispered. "I can't bear it."

She gave me a funny look, like she felt bad for me.

"I'm sorry," she said. "This is a dream and at some point I will wake up."

"Then dream it again," said Claire. "If it's a dream for you, dream it again."

"I'm not sure I can," I said. "I don't have any control over it."

Claire frowned. "Tell me. Tell me what you remember."

"Well—I guess it all started with the painting on my wall. A painting of your lighthouse. I've had it for months, but last night I couldn't sleep because I was worried about my mother, and I was staring at it and somehow—somehow—I must have fallen asleep and dreamed I walked into the painting, and there I was, on the road, looking up at your house."

"A painting? Of the lighthouse?"

"Yes, and I knew it was Newfoundland, so today I went to the library and found a book with Newfoundland paintings in it. There was another painting by the same artist of the lighthouse in a storm, and I guess I must have fallen asleep again, and I was outside, and I heard the screaming, and—and—and here I am."

"Weird," said Claire. "It doesn't sound like anything I ever heard about heaven or guardian angels or purgatory or—"

"Of course it isn't purgatory! It's Toronto! It's where I live. This—" I waved my arm around the room. "This is all a dream! I told you. It's just a dream, and you're in my dream, and when I wake up, you'll be gone."

"You won't be here, but that doesn't mean I will be gone. This is where I live, and it's not a dream. You're a ghost—a spirit. You're not alive. All the rest of your life is a dream, not this."

I stood up and my chair fell over backward.

"I am alive!" I protested. "I am not a ghost! This is a dream and you're the one who's not real. You're inside some painting in my imagination, and as soon as I wake up, you'll be gone."

Claire frowned again, as if she was trying to figure something out. Finally she looked up at me.

"Who did the paintings?" she asked. "Who's the artist who did the paintings of the lighthouse?"

"What does it matter? It's just some artist I never heard of her before—Maisie King, that's her name. Maisie King."

Claire stared at me. "What?"

"Maisie King. I don't know why I never heard of her, because she's really good. I've been studying Canadian painters with my teacher, but she's never come up. Maybe it's because—" I stopped. Claire was still staring at me, her eyes round.

"Maisie King is our mother," she whispered.

CLAIRE

ANNIE WASN'T THE same. She was mixed-up and angry, and of course she was older now, my age, not a four-year-old anymore. But she had changed. Annie was always running and jumping and coming up with wild stories and plans of things we could do, and I was always the one trying to slow her down. She was funny and mischievous and always tearing from one thing to another, never happy to sit still, unless she was drawing.

But now she was slow and cautious and scared—different. She was convinced that the life in her head in Toronto was real, and that she wasn't dead at all, and that she wasn't my sister. But the very fact that she came to me through Maisie's paintings proved something. Didn't it?

I stood up.

"Annie, look—" I began. But before I could say anything else, the house rattled in a strong gust of wind and the candle on the table between us flickered and went out, plunging the room into darkness. I counted to five and the beam from the lighthouse flashed through the room.

I was alone. Annie was gone.

ANNIE

THE CANDLE BLEW OUT and everything went dark. I waited for the beacon to flash on but nothing happened.

"What's going on?" I asked Claire.

There was no answer. Only darkness, all around me, thick and silent.

CLAIRE

THE WIND HAD picked up again and the Old Hollies came shrieking back around the corners of the house. I fumbled for the matches and relit the candle. I held it high so I could look into every corner of the room, but Annie was just as gone as she was before. I checked the front door to make sure it was closed tight and then took the candle up to my bedroom.

Maisie wouldn't leave Blackberry Bight till the worst of the storm was over. She might not be back for hours.

I wasn't scared. I liked being in the house by myself, and the Old Hollies didn't bother me anymore. Not now that I'd seen Annie and knew she wasn't a dream.

We kept an oil lamp in each room for power-outs. I took mine from the dresser and set it beside my bed and lit it. Then I blew out the candle and quickly got into my nightie and crawled under the covers. The house quivered and creaked in the wind, the rain drummed against the window and the waves pounded the shore. But I was safe and warm in a circle of light, high above the sea. Annie would be back. I knew it.

PART THREE

THE
DREAMER

"He's dreaming now," said Tweedledee:
"and what do you think he's dreaming about?"

Alice said "Nobody can guess that."

"Why, about you!" Tweedledee exclaimed,
clapping his hands triumphantly.
"And if he left off dreaming about you,
where do you suppose you'd be?"

"Where I am now, of course," said Alice.

"Not you!" Tweedledee retorted contemptuously. "You'd be
nowhere. Why, you're only a sort of thing in his dream!"

THROUGH THE LOOKING-GLASS,
AND WHAT ALICE FOUND THERE

ANNIE

"**A**RE YOU OKAY, DEAR?" asked a woman's voice.

I opened my eyes. I was in the library.

I felt a hand on my shoulder and looked up into Mrs. Silver's concerned face.

"You were asleep, Annie. Were you having a bad dream?"

"I—I think so," I said. My head felt fuzzy.

Mrs. Silver sat down beside me, placing the book she had been reading on the table. It was *Through the Looking-Glass*, one of my favorites. I'd known Mrs. Silver forever. She lived down the street and always had a kind word for me when I ran into her. I liked to pretend that if I ever had a grandmother she would be just like Mrs. Silver: there was something so comfortable and warm about her. She had silvery-white, curly hair, wire-rimmed glasses and soft blue eyes that crinkled up when she laughed, which was often. Her favorite colors must have been blue and gray, because I never saw her wearing any others.

Today she was wearing a soft blue cardigan over a gray dress.

The library was hushed around us. The path outside the windows was empty—the women with their strollers must have moved on. I glanced down at my knees. No blood. No scrapes. And my clothes were dry.

The Newfoundland art book still lay on the table in front of me, open to the picture of the lighthouse in the storm.

"That's a very good painting," said Mrs. Silver. "Where is it?"

"Newfoundland," I mumbled, and started to cry.

She sat down beside me, putting an arm round my shoulders.

"What's wrong?" She had such a gentle voice.

"My mother," I gulped. "She's in the hospital. I think she's going to die."

———

Somehow I ended up in the librarian's office, where they gave me water and tissues. I sat waiting and crying with Mrs. Silver patting my hand until Magda got there to take me home.

"Can you get me the book?" I asked Magda. "The book I was reading? I want to take it home."

The librarian stepped forward and handed me two books. "I've checked these out for you, dear," she said. "Now you take care of yourself and come back and see us soon."

"The poor thing," she said to Magda, whose face was tight with worry.

"I never should have let her go," she said to the librarian. "I would have stopped her, but I thought it might do her good to get out of the house, and I know she loves to go to the library, so I thought it would be fine, but I never should have let her go, the poor child." And she enveloped me in a hug. She smelled like vanilla.

"It's all just caught up with you, hasn't it?" Magda said, patting my back. "Never you mind now."

"I have to see Mom," I said, pulling away from her. "Please. Can we call my dad?"

———

We took a taxi to the hospital. Magda kept wringing her hands. I'd never seen anyone do that before. It was like she was washing them with invisible soap, over and over again.

"I can't bear hospitals," she muttered as we clambered out of the cab. "Ever since I was a girl and my father had pneumonia, and we thought he was going to die, and my mother took me to see him, and the smells and doctors in masks, and my poor father struggling for every breath he took—"

She stopped suddenly and looked down at me.

"He didn't die, though," she said quickly. "He lived to a ripe old age, down to the pub every Saturday night, happy as a clam."

She had my hand gripped tightly in hers as we went through the glass doors into the lobby and up to the reception desk.

Soon we were trundling down a long white hallway that seemed to go on forever. I couldn't see the end of it. It was lined with white tiles, and every few feet there was a closed door. We passed a few people going in the opposite direction. One old man was being pushed in a wheelchair by a nurse. Doctors dressed in green scrubs hurried along. I was finding it hard to breathe. Magda kept chattering on about her father and mother and Dublin, but I stopped listening.

Finally we turned off down a corridor and got in an elevator. It let us out on the fifth floor and we turned left. We had to go through some swinging doors and stopped at a tall counter, where Magda spoke to a nurse.

"This way," said the nurse, and led us down the hall and into a large room where each bed was blocked off by green curtains. She went up to one in the far corner and pulled back the curtains.

My stomach was flipping over and over. I loosened my hand from Magda's trembling grip and walked up to the bed. The curtains formed four walls, like a tent filled with a strange green light.

Mom lay there, motionless. The green light came from the screens behind her, with squiggly lines running up and down and across them. A tall pole with a plastic bag on it had a tube attached that ran under the covers.

Her eyes were closed. Her face was very white, except for a dark bruise on her cheek. Her chest rose and fell a little with each breath.

I stood staring at her, afraid to go any closer. Magda came in close behind me and gave me a little push.

"Go on. Speak to her," she whispered.

"But will she hear me?"

"I don't know. But she might. People always say you should talk to someone in a coma, that it does them good, whether they can hear every word or not."

I went forward then and laced my fingers through my mother's. They were cool.

"Mom?" I said. It came out like a croak. "Mom?"

She didn't move.

There was a scraping sound behind me as Magda moved a chair behind my legs. I sat down, still holding Mom's cool fingers in my hand.

"Mom?" I whispered. "Come back."

CLAIRE

MY MOTHER COMPLETELY freaked out when she saw the wet floor, the burned wall and the remains of the fire in the wood box. She came storming up the stairs and woke me up. I sat up, groggy with sleep.

"What happened?" she yelled, shaking me awake. "What did you do? How many times have I told you—"

"I—I—" My teeth chattered and I couldn't catch my breath.

"Tell me this instant!" she said, giving me another fierce shake.

I finally woke up completely. "Stop it!" I cried, pushing her hands away. "Let me tell you!"

She stood back, panting, her eyes wild and her hair all in a mess. She looked like a witch. Mary and Joan called her a witch sometimes, just to get a rise out of me, but the truth was she did look strange, compared to their proper mothers in their house-dresses and cardigans. Maisie wore long flowery skirts and big men's boots, with plaid lumber jackets layered over her hand-knit sweaters. She had long, curly dark-brown hair that expanded in the damp sea air like some strange dark halo. She wore a long black cloak that ballooned and swirled around her in the wind. The local women kept their distance, but all the men liked her fine.

Maisie had an awful temper. When she lost it, she raged and shouted and threw things and scared the life out of me. But I learned long ago that the only way to get through it was to keep my head down and wait till she blew herself out, like a storm at sea.

"The electricity went off. I lit a candle and the wind blew the door open and the wood box caught fire. I put it out with buckets of water and everything's fine. I'm fine."

She glared at me.

"How many times, Claire, how many times have I told you to be careful with candles, especially in storms? And the door should have been latched."

"If I latched it, how would you get in?"

"Through the lighthouse door. You must latch it in a storm. I've told you. When are you going to start taking responsibility? When are you going to grow up?"

"I was doing fine. It was an accident. Accidents happen."

"For some reason, they seem to happen around you more than anyone else."

She stopped, realizing what she had said. The room, the storm and the argument all fell away, and there was only Maisie and me and the horrible thing that we never talked about. It filled the space between us and seemed to suck all the air out of the room. We couldn't look away.

"It wasn't my fault . . ." I whispered. "She ran. I couldn't stop her."

"I didn't mean that," she said slowly. "You know I didn't mean that."

The silence deepened. It felt like we were standing on the edge of a precipice, and if we said anything else, we would lose our balance and fall.

Maisie closed her eyes and grabbed two fistfuls of hair on either side of her head, as if she could squeeze all the pain away. Then she opened her eyes and gave a big sigh.

"Claire, I'm sorry. I lost my temper. I was worried about you. I didn't mean anything else. Just go to sleep now, okay?"

I got back into bed. She waited until I pulled up the covers to my chin, then she left, closing the door behind her.

It's been hard between me and Maisie, ever since Annie died. She sent me away at first, to stay with Nan for a couple of weeks, after the accident. I heard her telling Nan she needed to be on her own, and Nan told her I needed her, and then Maisie said, "I can't face her. I just can't face her yet."

Then Nan said, "It wasn't her fault, Maisie. You know what Annie was like. None of us could hold her once she made up her mind to run."

"I know that," said Maisie. "Of course I know that. But I can't face her, just the same."

Annie was always Maisie's favorite. Mothers say they don't have favorites, but it was as plain as day. Annie was just like Maisie—lively and funny with a wicked temper and determined to get her own way. She and Maisie would have terrible shouting fights and then make up and roll around the floor laughing, while I stood by watching silently, forgotten. Annie loved to paint, just like Maisie, and would splash around happily with paint and brushes in Maisie's studio for hours, while it bored me silly. I'd rather read a book. I just don't see the world the way they did. They were always rushing to draw whatever they saw, while I—didn't.

Maisie would sigh and say, "What am I going to do with you, Claire?" when I refused to sit down and draw with the two of them, or yawned my way through another gallery opening. I hung back at parties, while Maisie and Annie would take the floor, dancing, laughing, both of them loving to be the center of attention. Sometimes people forgot that Maisie had two daughters, because Annie was so adorable and I was so quiet. Annie and I were fine on our own, but when Maisie was around, I felt like the odd one out.

Maisie told me many times that she didn't blame me for Annie's death. Too many times.

Every so often it comes out. What Maisie really feels. She'll let something slip about responsibility, or accidents, and I can see it in her eyes. She blames me all right.

Oh, she's tried to convince me that she doesn't. In those first few weeks she would go over it and over it, telling me it wasn't my fault. But I could tell by the way she looked at me that she blamed me. She thought I should have held tighter and I should have moved quicker to stop her.

But I didn't. The memory of that day is etched in my mind like a scene taken with a flash camera. Everything is bright and hard and clear. It was hot. Sammy started to bark and Annie was running across that road before I could blink. If it's anyone's fault, I guess it's Annie's. She knew not to run across the road; she knew she was supposed to hold my hand. But she loved that little dog and that's all she thought of.

How can one minute change everything so much, forever?

ANNIE

IT HAPPENED IN an instant. Mom was driving home from the university after teaching her Tuesday evening class when she lost control of the car somehow and ran into the concrete foundation of an overpass. They had to use the jaws-of-life, Dad said, to get her out. She was knocked unconscious by the force of the impact and never woke up. She had a severe concussion and lots of bruises. The airbag had saved her life, he said.

He was sitting at the kitchen table gulping down hot tea. Magda put another plate of peanut-butter, chocolate-chip muffins on the table. Dad had eaten two already and was soon halfway through his third. It was the morning after I saw Mom at the hospital. Magda had stayed overnight, sleeping on the couch in the living room.

Dad had spent all night at the hospital with Mom and just got home. He and Magda decided that I should stay home from school another day. Fine with me. I was tired, after a night of broken dreams about long hospital corridors and breaking glass.

Mom was at the hospital where Dad worked, so he knew a lot of the doctors and nurses in the intensive care unit. They kept him up to date about her condition.

"These coma cases can be tricky," he said, wiping some crumbs off his mouth with a linen napkin. "Cathleen doesn't seem to have any major injuries to her brain, aside from concussion, but they can't really tell yet. She could come out of it any time, or it could take a while. The good thing is, she's breathing on her own."

I watched his fingers as he folded the napkin carefully. They were long and thin. A surgeon's fingers. He operated on people's brains with those fingers. They hovered over the folded napkin, then reached for another muffin.

"The police don't understand why she lost control of the car," he went on, smearing butter on it. "There were no other cars around. They don't think she was going very fast."

I could see it in my mind: the dark road, the headlights of Mom's car, a dip in the road under a bridge—

"Maybe a cat—or a squirrel?"

He glanced over at me. There were dark shadows under his eyes. He held my gaze for a moment, as if he was about to tell me something, but all he said was, "Maybe."

———

A few minutes later, Dad went upstairs to get some sleep. We heard his footsteps as he slowly mounted the stairs, stumbling once and then continuing.

I pushed away my plate. Magda stood at the sink washing dishes and sighing loudly every now and then, but for once, not talking. The library books were sitting on the end of the table, where Magda must have left them when we got in from the hospital yesterday. I'd been so tired that I went to bed in the afternoon and fell into a deep sleep, waking up for the supper that Magda brought up to me on a tray, then promptly falling asleep again. This was my first chance to look at the book of Newfoundland painters again.

Through the Looking-Glass lay on top. Now how did that get there? It was the book Mrs. Silver had been looking at. The librarian must have thought it was one I wanted and checked it out by mistake.

It was one of my favorites. I couldn't resist flipping through to look at Tenniel's illustrations. Alice curled up with the kitten in the big chair, the frightful Jabberwock, the Red Queen running with Alice clutching her hand and flying out behind her. They were like old friends. There were Tweedledum and Tweedledee, and a few pages later, the Red King sleeping. I frowned. What did that remind me of? The Red King sleeping. I started to read. Then it came back to me.

Tweedledee told Alice that the Red King was dreaming the story and Alice was only a thing in his dream. Like Claire. She was just someone in my dream. When I stopped dreaming, she disappeared. But . . . but what if the dream wasn't mine? What if it was someone else's dream, and they were dreaming me?

I didn't like that idea. Not at all.

CLAIRE

I DON'T KNOW WHO my father is. Maisie won't tell.

"Somebody I knew at art school in Toronto," was all she would say. "Somebody unimportant."

How could the man who was my father be unimportant? I used to fantasize about him appearing at the door one day and taking me away to Toronto. He would be tall with straight, light-brown hair the same color as mine. I didn't look anything like Maisie or Annie, so I must look like him. He'd be rich, and lonely, and want me to come and live with him in a big house, and I'd have lots of nice clothes that weren't secondhand, and I'd have lots of friends and go to a cool high school in Toronto. Then I would travel the world—Ireland, France, Italy—all those places that lay on the other side of the wide Atlantic.

And I wouldn't give another thought to Maisie, or Crooked Head Lighthouse.

I knew it was a fantasy and that it would never happen. Not like that. My father, whoever he was, didn't even know he had a daughter. Maisie came back to St. John's after art school, found out she was pregnant and decided to go it alone. She never saw him again. It was the same with Annie's father. Maisie never told us who he was. I guess she thought he was as unimportant as my dad.

So I wasn't going to be rescued by my fantasy father. What would happen, though, was that I would get out of Crooked

Head Lighthouse someday, all by myself. And maybe sooner rather than later. I had a plan. Maisie didn't really want me with her. Every time she looked at me she saw the person who let Annie run.

Sometimes the silence in this house, between my mom and me, is so heavy that I feel I'm being ground into the floor. When I'm alone the silence is different—it's just quiet. My thoughts can run free and I'm almost happy. But when we're both here, there are so many things unsaid that they weigh me down.

I've never been much of a talker. Maisie and Annie would chatter away like birds, and I'd just listen to them. But after Annie died, Maisie's chitchat slowed down. It used to be when we drove in the car she kept up a running commentary on everything that was going on in her life—how her work was going, who was buying what painting and what she would charge them, all the doings of her friends, gossip and opinions about all their lives. I just tuned her out, like she was a radio in the background.

After Annie died our trips in the car were silent. She stopped sharing her thoughts with me. Strangely, I found I missed that. It was as if we drove out of range of the radio station, and the signal disappeared. Even though I hadn't really been listening, I felt its absence. She was just too far away for her voice to carry back to me.

ANNIE

I CLOSED *Through the Looking-Glass* and reached for the book about Newfoundland painters. The painting on the cover was of a huge whale under the ocean, with a wrecked ship plunging past it to the depths of the sea. I looked away. I sure didn't want to fall into that painting.

I focused on the lopsided green bow at the back of Magda's apron. Mom's apron. The last time Mom wore it was when she was making supper the night before the accident. She kept bugging me to set the table while I was trying to draw the salt and pepper shakers.

The image of her white, still face in the hospital swam into my head. My breath caught in my throat. It hurt, like something was trapped there. Where was she? How could she just not be here anymore? Was she aware of anything? Did it hurt? Or was she lost in a dream, unable to find her way back?

I couldn't bear thinking about her. I reached for the book. I turned the pages quickly to the Maisie King page and started reading about the artist.

Margaret Ellen ("Maisie") King was born in St. John's, Newfoundland, in 1944 and graduated from the Ontario College of Art in 1965. She made a living as a portraitist in St. John's for several years. In 1974 King moved to an abandoned lighthouse at Crooked Head, Newfoundland, where

her family had been lighthouse keepers for three genera-
tions. In this isolated spot, King developed her reputation
over the next decade as one of the foremost landscape artists in Newfoundland. Her portraits have also earned her
international kudos, and she has had numerous exhibits
of her paintings across North America and in Europe. She
still lives and works at Crooked Head Lighthouse.

No mention of any daughters, dead or alive. But it said
Maisie moved to the lighthouse in 1974. And Claire said they
had moved there right after her sister died, four years before.

I was dreaming about the past. When I saw Claire, it was
1978. I did a quick sum in my head: 2004 minus 1978 was
twenty-six years ago.

I looked up. Magda was rummaging in a cupboard, pulling
out flour and baking soda. She was probably going to make
more muffins. Her motto seemed to be, "When in doubt, bake."
Fine with me, if only I had an appetite. Through the window, I
could see the sun dappling through the leaves on the tree in the
backyard. Everything was normal. Except for me.

What was wrong with me? Why had I fallen asleep in the
library in the middle of the morning? And why was I dreaming
of things that happened so long ago? How did Maisie King's
painting get into my attic? And the quilt?

I looked back at the book. The next picture was the one of the
lighthouse in the storm. I flipped past it and opened my eyes just

a little bit to squint at the new page. Then I forgot about trying to keep myself from falling into the pictures and just stared.

It was a painting of me in my blue cotton pajamas, my hair wild about my face.

My mouth felt dry and I felt that empty, dropping feeling you get when you think your heart has suddenly stopped—and then it started pounding like crazy, ringing in my ears. How did my picture get into this book? I looked at the caption—it was called *Annie III*, and the date was 1978. Then I looked more closely at the painting.

The pajamas weren't my pajamas, but they were the same shade of blue, with little white flowers all over them. Mine had yellow flowers. Her hair was the same curly dark-brown as mine, but longer, and her features, as far as I could see, were almost identical to mine, except she was a few years younger than me. The only thing that wasn't exactly what I saw in the mirror every morning was her expression. Her eyes were alight with mischief, and she had a big grin on her face. I was sure I never smiled liked that. She was bursting with life—as if she was going to jump out of the painting and go running around the room.

Just as I thought that, looking into her dancing eyes, the room started spinning and I felt like I was falling. I closed my eyes tight to try and stop it, but it didn't work.

The first thing I noticed was the sweet, salty smell of the ocean air. Then I heard the waves rolling in on the rocks below the lighthouse. I opened my eyes.

I was standing in a room stacked with paintings, with a dresser crowded with paint tubes against one wall and a fireplace with a chimney against the other. A table with more tubes and paintbrushes stood beside an easel—and on the easel was the painting of the girl in the blue pajamas. The other Annie.

CLAIRE

THE MORNING AFTER the storm, Maisie went out to the store and I wandered into her studio. I don't often venture over the threshold. It's her private space, and she doesn't like people looking at her work before it's finished. But I glide through it every once in a while, just to see what she's up to. I don't touch anything, so she doesn't know I've been in there.

I don't really understand most of her paintings. She does landscapes and portraits. The landscapes are thick with color and it's not the way I see things. It's the same with the portraits—I can recognize the people she's drawing, but she brings out unexpected expressions or their features are slightly skewed, and I don't get it. Like one she did of her friend Tilly, who is a loud, laughing actor who always has a joke or something outrageous to tell you. In the portrait, Tilly's eyes were on a slant and her mouth turned down. She looked sad. Not how she looks in real life.

That morning, after the storm, I was looking for one picture in particular. I went to her easel and caught my breath.

There it was. A picture of Annie in her blue pajamas. The same pajamas she was wearing the night she came to my bedroom.

ANNIE

T HE PAINTING LOOKED just as it did in the book, only much more vibrant. I took a step closer. There was a black toy Scottie dog lying on a bed behind the girl.

A breath of wind ruffled my hair and I looked up. Light poured in the windows and I could see a blue sky with white clouds scudding across it in a stiff wind. The wide ocean spread out to a thin line on the horizon.

"Annie," whispered a voice in my ear.

I spun around and there was Claire, right behind me. She spread her arms wide and enveloped me in a tight hug. She felt soft and smelled like the lavender sachet in my sock drawer.

"I knew you'd come back," she said.

For a moment I wanted to stay in the circle of that hug. I felt something that was tight in my chest start to give a little.

"You don't feel like a ghost," she said, with a little laugh. "I can feel your heart beating."

I pulled away.

"I'm dreaming again," I said stiffly. I moved over to the easel. "I saw this painting in a book and I fell asleep and here I am."

Claire frowned. "You couldn't have seen it in a book. Maisie doesn't show the Annie pictures to anyone. Not even me. I just sneak in here and look at them without her knowing."

"There are more paintings of Annie?" I asked.

Claire nodded.

"Every year," she said, her voice not quite steady. "Every year around the anniversary of the accident, she paints you. This is her latest. She just painted it this week."

My stomach felt like it was dropping away.

"When . . . When is the anniversary of the accident?"

Claire stared at me. "June 10," she whispered. "Two days ago."

The day my mother crashed her car.

I swallowed. Claire's eyes seemed to be boring into mine. They were dark blue, like blueberries. I knew those eyes. I looked away. I felt like I was falling again.

"Do you want to see them?" she said. "The paintings?"

"Uh . . . okay."

She turned on her heel and led me out into the hall, then crossed to a door on the opposite wall that stood at the head of the stairs.

"Through here," she said, opening it.

I followed her in and found myself in the biggest closet I had ever seen. It ran down the whole side of the house, with shelves and drawers along one side, and hooks and bars to hang clothes on down the other. It was full of clothes and blankets and sheets and pillowcases and towels.

Claire walked swiftly to a door at the other end of the closet. "This leads to the other side," she said, and pushed it open.

"Other side? Of what?" I asked.

"Of the house," she said, and stepped through the door.

It was a mirror house: everything was the same but reversed. The stairs ran down to the left, and three doors stood along the hallway.

"There used to be two families here," said Claire. "Nan's family on our side and the Pierceys on the other. Mr. Piercey was the assistant lighthouse keeper. Nan and her brothers and sisters used to play with Mr. Piercey's kids when they were little. Nan told us lots of stories about it. We always called it the Mirror House." She glanced over at me, as if she was testing me to see if I remembered.

I didn't say anything, but I felt uneasy. Why did the words *mirror house* come to me before Claire even said it? I was thinking about how Alice went through the looking glass and everything was backward. Anyone would think that. It wasn't because I remembered anything. I'd never been here before.

I followed Claire into the middle room.

"Maisie keeps paintings over here. We're not really supposed to use it; we only pay rent for the other side, but no one has come here for years and years, so Maisie uses it for her stuff. And I come over sometimes."

She watched me as I looked around the room.

"You really don't remember, do you?" she said.

"I've never been here before." It had been a bedroom, and an iron bedstead still stood in one corner, covered in a threadbare quilt, but the rest of the room was stacked with canvases. The window looked south over a sparkling blue sea and dark-green headlands running into the distance.

"We used to come in here with Nan, years ago. You were just little. I guess that's why you don't remember," said Claire, crossing to some canvases in the far corner. "Maisie puts her paintings over here when she's done. If she doesn't sell them, sometimes she paints over them. Or just leaves them." She started moving the paintings at the front of the stack aside.

My fingers were twitching. I wanted to see all the paintings in that room, right away.

"She keeps all the Annie paintings hidden back here." Claire started hauling canvases over to the window. "Come and look," she said, setting three against the wall, where they were illuminated by the light from the window. She stood back to look at them, then stepped forward again and rearranged them. "Now they're in order. Starting with the year you would have been five, up to this year, when you would have been eight. That's the one in the studio. The new one."

I caught my breath. The paintings showed the girl on a street, in front of the lighthouse, baking cookies—laughing, happy, full of life. She could have been my identical twin.

CLAIRE

THE FIRST TIME I saw one of the Annie paintings was on the first anniversary of her death, June 10, 1975. I wandered into Maisie's studio while she was away at the store, and there was Annie grinning out at me from the easel, standing in front of our old house in St. John's, holding a little black Scottie dog in her arms.

It knocked the breath out of me for a minute. Annie looked like she was going to leap out of the painting and come running toward me, calling out that she'd caught Sammy and the car had missed her. I felt like I'd been slammed by a car myself, with the shock of seeing her like that. When I caught my breath, I walked closer to the painting.

She was different. She was older. Her face was a little thinner, her hair was longer and she was bigger all over—as if she'd aged a year since I saw her last.

I heard the door slam downstairs as Maisie came into the house, and I skedaddled out of there on my tiptoes so she wouldn't hear me.

I haunted the studio for the next few months, whenever Maisie was out, looking for more pictures of Annie. But there was nothing. The next June on the anniversary of Annie's death, I crept into Maisie's studio when she was out for a walk, and there was Annie, beaming out at me, standing in front of the lighthouse in a red knitted sweater with the image of a black

Scottie worked into it. Annie had changed again and looked like a sturdy little girl of six.

After that I always went looking in June and I always found a new Annie picture. Sometimes on the easel, sometimes hidden away among other paintings. In each one she was older, and Sammy was always in the painting. Last year's painting featured Annie mixing cookie dough at our kitchen table with a china Scottie dog standing on the window ledge behind her. This year's had Annie standing in her old bedroom in St. John's, with a stuffed toy Scottie dog on the bed behind her.

Maisie never sold those paintings or showed them anywhere. I don't think anyone in the world knew about them except me. She was painting Annie as if she was still alive, growing up, but always with that little black dog there to remind us of the accident.

They gave me the creeps.

ANNIE

I SANK DOWN ON the bed and stared at the pictures. My five-, six- and seven-year-old selves smiled back. It was me: from the dark, slightly crooked eyebrows to the stubby fingers to the wayward curl escaping over my forehead. I had done enough self-portraits in my art class to know my features inside out, and they were all there. Only the eyes were different. Same color, same shape, but the light of mischief wasn't mine. This Annie looked like she would be bouncing all the time, seldom sitting still, never measuring her words before they left her mouth.

Something caught in my throat. This was the way I might have been, if I hadn't grown up in such a cool, ordered house, with parents who frowned when they looked at me, where I was always careful not to show too much. If I had grown up here, with that vast sky and ocean all around me, a big sister to play with and a mother who knew about painting . . .

And she did know. Despite the shock of seeing these paintings of a dead girl who looked just like me, part of my brain was busily assessing the technique. I had been drawn to Maisie King's landscapes, but her portraits were something else again—brilliant, but unsettling. Like she saw something her subjects might not want shown. Here it was a slight self-satisfaction. This little girl was loved, and happy, and she felt she could do whatever she wanted without consequence.

There was a simmering anger behind these paintings. At the girl, at the dog. I shook my head, as if coming up for air.

CLAIRE

ANNIE SAT ON the bed, staring at the paintings for a long time. She seemed to be lost in them. She looked at them just the way Maisie did when she was particularly interested in a painting. Like she was a million miles away. Somewhere I could never follow. Suddenly she shook her head and took a deep breath.

"Annie," I said. No reaction. "ANNIE!" I said, again, louder.

She turned toward me and slowly her eyes came into focus. "Your mother is one good painter," she said. "Amazing."

I felt something hot inside my chest, rising up into my face.

"OUR mother," I snapped. "Our mother is a good painter, yes. But that's beside the point. She could be the greatest painter in the world and I couldn't care less. She's a lousy mother."

I stomped over and started grabbing the paintings and putting them back where they came from.

"For the last four years, our mother has spent hours painting these weird, sicko pictures of you while she ignores me for days on end." I shoved the paintings behind the others. "I hate it here. I have no friends. I'm lonely. But she doesn't care. She tells me to try harder and then disappears into her studio for hours. Painting. You're more important to her than I am. You always were. And now painting you is more important to her than talking to me. About anything."

Annie sat very still, watching me.

"All I want is out of here. As soon as I can, I'm moving in with Nan and if I never see Maisie again, I don't care. She won't even notice I'm gone." A sob bubbled up and I took a deep breath. "And when I grow up, I'm going to get as far away as I can from this godforsaken place and never come back."

Annie started. "What? What did you say?"

"I said I'm going to get as far away from this godforsaken place as I can, where it rains all the time and everyone knows your business, and I'm never coming back."

Annie just kept staring at me, like I was the ghost.

"Claire," she said in a shaky voice. "What's your name? Your full name?"

"You know my name."

"No. I don't. Please tell me."

"Claire King," I said. "Claire Cathleen Morrow King."

Annie stood up. She was trembling.

"I have to get out," she said, pushing past me to the door. "I can't breathe."

She stumbled out the door and racketed down the stairs.

She ran the way Annie always ran—without warning and quick as a flash of light. One minute she was there beside me and the next she was gone, the front door banging shut behind her.

I let her go. I took one last look around the room to make sure it looked the same as it did when we came in, then I slipped back through the closet into our side of the house. I went to my room and stood looking out the window over the downs. I thought I caught a glimpse of Annie's red shorts flickering as she ran through the woods.

I stood watching, and sure enough, she emerged at the far end and stood at the edge of the cliff, looking out to the ocean. I sighed. I thought Annie coming back would fix everything. But it wasn't going to be that simple.

ANNIE

I FORGOT WE WERE in the Mirror House and halfway down the stairs I had this weird feeling that not only was everything inside me off-kilter, but that the house was turning itself inside out. I pulled up and nearly fell, but grabbing the bannister saved me. I could see an empty kitchen through one door and an empty living room through the other. I got to the front door, yanked it open, ran down the steps and took off around the house. The road to the shore curved off to the left and ahead of me a rough path led up over the hill.

I slipped on a rock, but managed to right myself, and ran up the path. I couldn't hear Claire behind me but I didn't want to stop and check. I just kept running, jumping over rocks and trying not to fall on the uneven ground. That tilting feeling was worse than ever and my head was spinning. I felt like I was falling as I ran, slipping down a slope, running into a place I didn't want to go, into something I couldn't understand.

The path took me through a woods—not what we'd call a woods in Ontario, just clumps of trees not much bigger than I was—up and down little rises, twisting around corners, then out into the open again.

I stopped, panting. I was at the far edge of the point, with rocks below and the blue ocean stretching on before me. There was nowhere to go from here. Except back. The world stopped tilting. I took a deep breath and looked around me.

It seemed like I could see forever. I turned in a slow circle. The lighthouse stood over to my right, high above the sea. A long strip of land curved back toward the mainland, where rocky headlands inched out to the horizon in both directions. The ocean surrounded me on three sides, with the sunshine spreading a wide arc of diamond sparkles across the surface.

It was the most beautiful place I'd ever been. The vast sky cupped over the world and I spread out my arms to it. The place was welcoming me, holding me up, giving me strength. I didn't understand anything about what was happening. Nothing made sense except this huge, breathtaking world I was standing in. In the midst of all my confusion I was only certain of one thing. I had come home.

CLAIRE

THE FRONT DOOR slammed. I turned my head away from the window.

"Claire, I'm home," called my mother.

I looked back at the headland. Annie was gone.

PART FOUR

THE
SECRET

"That's the effect of living backwards," the Queen
said kindly: "it always makes one a little giddy at first—"

The White Queen, THROUGH THE LOOKING-GLASS,
AND WHAT ALICE FOUND THERE

ANNIE

"ANNIE!"

Somebody was shaking me.

I opened my eyes and looked up into my father's worried face.

"Annie, what's wrong? Why do you keep falling asleep?"

"Whaaa?" I said groggily, sitting up and looking around. I was at the kitchen table, the book about Newfoundland artists in front of me, opened to the page with the girl in the blue pajamas. I shut the book quickly. Magda stood behind my father, wringing her hands again.

"Oh dear, oh dear, oh dear," she kept saying, over and over again.

"Magda, please," said my father. "Try to calm down. She's okay."

She gave one little squeak and then bit down on her lips. He turned back to me, took my hand in his and laid his fingers on my pulse, glancing at his watch.

We sat there for a moment or two, my heart pounding in my ears. Then he let go and leaned down to look into my face.

"How do you feel?" he said in his doctor's voice. It was noticeably different than his regular voice—much less impatient, concerned but cool—like I was some patient he didn't know who had just walked into his office with a problem he could solve.

I hated his doctor voice.

"Ummm, I'm a bit dizzy," I said. "And I'm tired."

"Your pulse is fast," he said. "I think there might be something going on with you that we should look into. This isn't normal, falling asleep like this, first in the library, now here. I'm thinking acute narcolepsy, although it's come on very suddenly." He was muttering away, almost as if he was talking to himself, not me. "Are you having any hallucinations?"

"Hallucinations?"

"Dreams, visions. Are you seeing things while you're sleeping?"

I stared at him. I didn't want to tell him about the paintings, the lighthouse, Claire—he'd have me in the hospital before I could blink.

"Not really," I said. "I'm just tired, Dad. I'm worried about Mom."

My upper lip trembled and I felt that breathless feeling I always get when I'm trying not to start crying. Dad frowned and Magda hovered behind him, clucking to herself like a hen.

Dad cleared his throat. "Of course you are. Shock. It could be just shock." It was still his doctor's voice, but a muscle under his skin on his jawline was jumping up and down. "I think perhaps she should go to bed for a while, Magda. We'll just keep an eye on this, Annie, but if it doesn't stop we'll have to get you in for some tests." He stood up. "I'm heading back to the hospital. I'll keep in touch."

He left the room swiftly. Magda put her arm around my shoulders and gave me a squeeze.

"She'll be fine, sweetie, you'll see," she said. "She'll wake up soon and be her old self. Don't you worry."

I looked up at her.

"I don't want tests," I said. "I hate tests."

———

Just because my father was a doctor, he seemed to think he could send me for tests whenever he felt like it. Whenever he couldn't figure me out. Which was often.

Why wasn't I talking more, why wasn't I doing better at school, why did I have no friends, why did I just want to draw all the time? He was always sending me off for tests, and I was always slipping away from being pinned down with any of the conditions he thought I might have.

Learning disabilities—no. Autism—no, Asperger's—no, social malfunction—no. I learned a lot about all kinds of things that can go wrong with kids, just by listening to what the psychologists and doctors and specialists said while they were testing me, and eavesdropping on my parents when they were talking about me. I would creep into my clothes closet after they thought I was asleep and listen to them talking in their bedroom next door. My closet was separated from their closet by a thin wood partition, so I could hear them quite clearly.

Apparently I was a very unsatisfactory child. I didn't care about schoolwork and my marks weren't good. The tests showed I was intelligent, so they couldn't figure out why I wasn't doing better. All I wanted to do was draw. One of the psychologists suggested they should encourage me, so they reluctantly started sending me to art classes downtown every Saturday morning. That was the only good result that ever came out of a test.

I had a picture book when I was little, one of the ones my mom had banished to the attic, about a changeling child that was substituted for a real baby. He was ugly and odd-looking and sat staring at the world with a blank expression. Sometimes I thought maybe I was a changeling, a strange, unnatural baby someone substituted for my parents' real child. That would explain why I felt so out of step with them, like I was living in my own world and I needed a translator to communicate with them.

And now Dad thought I might have a brand-new disease, narco-something. After Magda left me tucked up in bed, I waited till I heard her go downstairs, then I crept down the hall to Dad's study. He had a medical dictionary in there and whenever they were testing me for a new condition I would secretly go and look it up.

Narcolepsy: a condition characterized by brief attacks of deep sleep often occurring with cataplexy and hypnagogic hallucinations.

I didn't know what *cataplexy* or *hypnagogic* meant, but the rest of it sounded like what was happening to me. Sudden deep sleeps and hallucinations that I could walk inside paintings and end up in Newfoundland.

I tiptoed out into the hall and listened. Magda was humming to herself in the kitchen. I edged along the hall and into my parents' room. The bed was unmade. That never happened. Dad must have left his sheets and blankets in a tangle when Magda called him to help try and wake me up.

My mother's purse sat on her dressing table. I walked over and undid the zip. It was a black leather purse with different compartments. Ever since I was a very little girl, I loved going into my mother's purse. I could only look in with her permission, and every so often she said yes. There were usually wrapped butterscotch candies at the bottom, in a tangle with handkerchiefs that smelled like her perfume, her good silver pen, a lipstick. Her red leather wallet.

I pulled it out. Her driver's license was visible in the plastic window on one side. Under her driver's license were all my school pictures. I liked digging them out and sorting through them, going back to kindergarten, remembering this dress or that blouse, looking at my different haircuts. I wanted to pull out the pictures and compare them to the paintings I had seen of Little Annie, but I needed to see the license first. There was her name in capital letters, printed across the top: Cathleen Morrow Jarvis.

No Claire. She must have dropped that at some point. And King. My mother always told me her maiden name was Morrow.

I stared at her picture. It was new, taken earlier that year, near her birthday. Straight, light-brown hair cut in a pixie cut, close to her head and neat as a pin. Dark blueberry-blue eyes that looked out sadly on the world. The little frown lines on her forehead, that made her look as if she was always worried.

My mom. Claire. Claire grown up.

CLAIRE

I WATCHED THE HEADLAND for a while, and the woods, but there was no flash of Annie's red shorts. She was gone. But she'd be back. I knew that. I knew deep inside that no matter what she said about her other life, she was my Annie and she was here to help me. Help me get out of Crooked Head and the half-life I'd been living ever since she died.

I could hear Maisie banging around downstairs, putting groceries away. I sat down in the big chair by the window and gazed out at the ocean sparkling in the sunshine.

I closed my eyes. My head ached. It had been aching for days. It was almost time for me to put my plan into action, and I was scared. Scared it wouldn't work.

I had had my plan for a long time. It started way back when we first moved here.

I was always good at schoolwork. I like the neatness of it. You have a list of questions and you answer them. It's all laid down in black and white. And I always liked doing my homework.

It was something that was mine, and something that made sense when everything around me was in chaos. Maisie was never much of a housekeeper, and there was always a jumble of clothes and books and newspapers all over the place. But my room is tidy, and everything has its place. I do my homework at my desk, where I can look out over the ocean when I'm thinking about an answer.

I do my homework twice: once in rough and then once in good. Sometimes twice in good if I'm not happy with the first version. I spend hours on it. When I was in grade four, the first year we moved here, my mother went to talk to my teacher on Parent-Teacher Night, and she told her she thought I got too much homework, and that a child my age shouldn't be spending two hours a night at it.

My teacher that year was Mrs. Bartlett, who was cheery and quick, and never spent much time looking at you when she talked.

"Two hours?" she asked, with a laugh. "Mrs. King, two hours?" (They all called Maisie "Mrs." and she finally stopped correcting them. Seems that if you had a child, you automatically became a "Mrs.," no matter what.) "She gets half an hour's homework at the most. She does a lovely job on it, but it's not my responsibility if she spends two hours doing it."

"I just don't think she should have to work that hard," said my mother. "She should have time to play."

Mrs. Bartlett laughed again, a short, sharp laugh like it was shot from a gun. "Claire is the most serious child I've ever known. Does she even know how to play? I think you should just leave her be and let her find her own way."

I sat silently beside my mother.

"You enjoy your schoolwork, don't you, Claire?" said Mrs. Bartlett to me.

"Yes," I said.

"There now, nothing to worry about," she said.

I kept at it over the years. I wouldn't go to sleep until my homework was perfect. I got great marks. Not that it did me any good, except with Nan, who was always proud of me. But Maisie would skim her eyes over my report card and say, "All As again. When are you going to start having fun, Claire?" then put it aside and go back to whatever she was doing. The kids at school weren't impressed either. They called me Teacher's Pet and added my high marks to the list of things that made me a weirdo: my townie accent, my secondhand clothes, my fatherless state.

I didn't care. I read books at recess and ignored them. I kept up with my perfect homework. And I started to plan my escape.

ANNIE

I THINK I KNEW the whole time. Right from the moment I heard that voice calling, "Annie," the night of the accident. And when I saw her in her room in the moonlight, staring at me after she screamed. I knew, but I didn't know. Something deep inside me recognized something in her, but I couldn't quite grasp it, not until she said that thing about wanting to get away from Newfoundland where it rains all the time and everyone knows your business. That was my mother's voice, telling me what she'd told me so many times before.

Taking her wallet and her purse with me, I stumbled back into my room and got into bed. I sat with the purse in my lap and looked at the painting of Newfoundland hanging on my wall. It was ordinary now—no moonlight, no birds winging their way across the sky, no waving grasses. Everything was still.

My mother. Claire Cathleen Morrow King. Thirty-eight years old, lying in the hospital, hooked up to machines. And somehow at the same time, twelve years old and pacing back and forth in her room in the Crooked Head Lighthouse, plotting to get away. Was she dreaming all of it? Trying to work something out that happened long ago? But where did I come into it? How did I get into her dreams?

Could I possibly be her little sister who died? A ghost, like Claire said? But that was silly. I wasn't a ghost. I pinched my leg, hard. It hurt. I was too solid to be a ghost. But could I have possibly been Little Annie in another life? Reincarnation: the belief that people are born again and again into different lives. We studied it at school in World Religions. Hindus believed in reincarnation. And a few other religions did too. I liked the idea because it meant that your spirit never really died, but kept on living. You might know your loved ones in another life, but you don't remember them. You don't remember anything about your former life. Maybe that's what happened to me. I died in the accident, but then I was born again as Claire's daughter, so I came back into her life.

I shook my head. No. I didn't want to be Little Annie, hit by a car. I was me. Claire was my mother. I shook my head again. I felt as if my life was starting to slip away and I wasn't certain about anything. I had to figure it out. Somehow.

I fumbled in the wallet under the license, drew out the collection of my school pictures and spread them on the quilt. I put them in order, the way Claire had done with the paintings. There were seven: kindergarten to grade six.

In the first one I was five. My dark-brown hair fluffed out around my face. I was serious, and looked a little scared. I remembered how worried I was that day they took the pictures. I didn't like being with strangers who talked in such big jolly voices to me. But despite my wary expression, I looked just like Little Annie in her five-year-old picture. The same fat cheeks, the same mouth and eyes.

I shivered, then picked up the next one, when I was six, in

grade one, and the one from grade two. My face was identical to Little Annie's in the paintings. I could have been her.

I gathered the pictures up and fit them in behind the license again. Then I lay down and held the purse tight to my chest, under the blue-and-white quilt.

What was happening to me?

I could hear Magda downstairs in the kitchen, rattling the dishes, opening and closing cupboard doors, humming to herself the way she always did when she was working, snatches of Irish folk songs or pop songs from the radio. My window was open, and every so often I heard a car going by, or a dog barking, or kids' voices rising and falling as they walked by the house. It was a normal June afternoon in Toronto, and I was lying in bed with my mother's purse as the world spun out of control.

CLAIRE

IN GRADE FOUR my plan was to work really hard at my school-work so I could get a scholarship and go far, far away to university. On the mainland. And never come back. It seemed such a long way off, but I kept at it. By the time I got to grade six, I started wondering if I could go to high school in St. John's and get away even sooner. Nan was always telling Maisie that the schools out here aren't as good as the ones in St. John's. She's never given up trying to get Maisie to move back to town. She misses us.

The only part of my plan I hadn't quite figured out was how to persuade Maisie to let me go and live with Nan. Unlike Nan, I knew I'd never get Maisie to leave Crooked Head. She loved it too much and her work had been exploding ever since we moved here. She'd had shows in St. John's and Montreal and Toronto and was starting to make a name for herself. And according to Maisie it was all because she was living and painting in Crooked Head. It "fed her art," that's what she told me and Nan, again and again. Maybe that was true. But it didn't feed me. I was starving.

I figured I had lots of time to come up with something so Maisie would let me go. But then last November, everything changed.

I was in grade seven, but our class was mixed—half grade seven and half grade eight—taught by Mrs. Matchim. She is very stern and hardly ever cracks a smile. But she took notice back in the fall that I was getting high 90s on all my tests, and in November on Parent-Teacher Night she spoke to my mom about it.

"Mrs. King, Claire needs more of a challenge. She's ahead of the other students and the work is too easy for her."

"Yes," said my mother, glancing sideways at me. "I know."

"I propose that I start giving her the grade eight work. She should be able to catch up with it and then she could graduate into high school next fall."

"I don't know . . ." said my mother. "That would mean changing schools next year, and she'd be with kids who are a year older than she is."

"Yes, but she'd have work that was more suited to her capabilities. You don't want to hold her back, do you?"

"No, of course not." Maisie looked at me again. "Well, Claire?"

I swallowed. A wave of excitement was rising up inside me. Grade eight work! Skip grade seven! I'd be in high school next year! And maybe . . . maybe . . . maybe in St John's!

"I would like that," I said carefully.

"It will be double the homework," said Mrs. Matchim.

Maisie rolled her eyes. "She'll love that, won't you, Claire?"

I allowed myself to smile. "Yes," I said. I pictured myself sitting at my desk, books piled up around me, filling in pages and pages in my notebooks, with my neat writing all in tidy rows, with little red A+s scattered here and there.

That's when I really started to work hard. Mrs. Matchim gave me extra assignments every night, so I could catch up with all the work the grade eight students had done since September.

For the first time since I came to Crooked Head, I was almost happy. I was staying up till eleven or twelve o'clock every night and putting in long hours on the weekends. And daydreaming about how I would go to high school in St. John's next September.

Only I still didn't know how I was going to get Maisie to say yes.

ANNIE

I SAT UP, MY HEAD whirling with images of Little Annie, Claire, the lighthouse and the ocean stretching out to the sky. Maybe it was all just a dream. Maybe I was having those hallucinations that people with narcolepsy had? And because I loved the painting so much, I dreamed about going inside it. And because I was so worried about Mom, I was dreaming about her as a little girl. Maybe none of it was true.

But it was all so real. If I closed my eyes, I could still feel the wind on my face as I stood on the point looking out at the endless ocean.

I had to find out what was going on. But where to start?

I looked at the painting of Newfoundland hanging on my wall. The red lighthouse stood stark against the sky.

The painting. When I found it, it had been wrapped in the quilt. And there had been a shabby old trunk in front of it, in the corner of the attic, under the eaves. I guess it had always been there, but I'd never given it a second thought. Till now.

I stood at the door and listened. Magda had the radio on low, and I could hear dishes clanging. I walked to the end of the hall, opened the door that led to the attic and went up.

The attic was dusty and dim, even with the light on. There were old dressers, suitcases, boxes of Christmas decorations, my picture books. And in the far corner, half-hidden behind a dismantled table, stood the trunk.

I moved the table top away and looked at it. It was about three feet long and two feet high, dark red with wooden slats across. There was a brass hasp at the front—and a padlock. It was locked.

I sat back on my heels. There had to be a key somewhere. And I thought I knew where.

I crept silently down the stairs and into Mom's room. I sat down at her dressing table and reached for her green velvet jewelry box. As I did, I caught sight of my reflection in the three-fold mirror. My hair was all over the place, my face was deathly pale and my eyes looked wild. I looked so much like Little Annie that I caught my breath.

Not Little Annie. Her ghost. In all the images of her in Maisie's paintings she was always cheery. She never looked this sad and desperate. I took a deep breath.

"You're not Little Annie's ghost," I muttered to myself, looking firmly into my own eyes in the mirror. "You're Annie Jarvis and your mother is sick and you're going to get to the bottom of this."

Then I tore my eyes away from my sad reflection and bent my head over the jewelry box.

Like my mother's wallet, it was one of those places I never got tired of exploring. It had three tiers that came forward as I raised the lid. Little compartments for rings, brooches, necklaces, bracelets. Mom was very neat about everything, and her jewelry was perfectly organized. It was simple and modern—some silver and some gold. But at the very bottom was a larger area where she put costume jewelry that she hardly ever wore, and that was always my favorite part of the box, because it was bright and gaudy and fun to try on.

I pulled out everything that was there, and sure enough, right at the bottom was a key. I'd remembered seeing it a few times. Mom said it was just an old key and she couldn't remember what it was for. I should have known she was lying: Mom always knew what everything was for and anything that was old or forgotten was either thrown out or relegated to the attic.

I replaced the costume jewelry in the box, closed it, and then went back up to the attic, the key clutched tight in my hand.

I knew it would fit.

CLAIRE

THE SCHOOL IN Crooked Head only went to grade eight. Once you graduated, you had to go on a forty-five-minute bus ride to Lattice Harbour for high school. It wasn't a very good school. Maisie's friends who lived along the coast closer to St. John's drove their kids into the city for high school. But we were too far away to drive in every day.

There was a good high school near Nan's: St. Brigid's Collegiate. If I went and lived with Nan, I could go there. And I could go back to Crooked Head some weekends, or Maisie could come into town. She came in anyway once or twice a month. What would be the big deal about that?

But I knew Maisie wouldn't see it that way. Even though she went for days without really seeing me and barely speaking to me, I had a feeling she wouldn't want to let me go. I had to do really well this year and maybe get Mrs. Matchim on my side. If she told Maisie I needed to go to the high school in St. John's, that might help. I knew Nan would love it if I came and lived with her, but she'd just say, "It's up to your mother," and try not to get involved in any conflict between Maisie and me.

I kept meaning to talk to Mrs. Matchim, but I kept putting it off. Thinking, just wait till after the Easter exams and see how well I do. I did just fine in those exams, but still I didn't ask her. I don't know why. So then I thought I'd wait till after the end-of-year exams and see how I did. Now they were over and I was waiting for my results. But I knew I'd done really well. I only had two weeks before the end of school. I had to ask her soon.

The longer I put off talking to Maisie about it, the harder it was to bring it up. I told myself I'd talk to Mrs. Matchim at recess Monday morning. And if she didn't back me up, then I'd talk to Maisie myself.

And maybe I'd see Annie again before that. And she'd help me. No matter how different she was, just knowing she was close by made me feel better. I smiled. Annie.

The sun was streaming in the window, bathing me in a warm golden glow. I could almost fall asleep, here in the chair, with the soft ocean breeze on my face. And maybe if I slept, my head would feel better.

ANNIE

THE KEY FIT. I knew it would. I flipped the hasp open and raised the lid.

The trunk was full of presents. Wrapped in Christmas paper with puffins wearing bright red scarves and mittens. Wrapped in bright birthday paper with smiling whales. Presents. I picked up one and looked at it. "To Annie, on her eleventh birthday," said the label. "From Gran."

I didn't have a gran. My father's parents died before he met Mom.

I picked up a present wrapped in green paper with little Christmas trees all over it. The label read, "Merry Christmas, Annie, from Gran." Then I pulled out the presents, one by one, and laid them on the dusty floor in two rows.

Twelve birthday presents. Twelve Christmas presents. All for me, from "Gran."

There were other things in the trunk: a red woolen blanket and some books and papers, but I left them for the moment and turned to the presents.

I picked up the one that said "Happy First Birthday, Annie." As I unpeeled the tape, I noticed that it had been unwrapped before, and then carefully rewrapped. I looked at a couple of others; they were the same. Mom had unwrapped these presents, looked inside, and then wrapped them up again, trying not to make it show. Why? Why hadn't she given them to me?

I turned back to the "Happy First Birthday" present and removed the paper. There was a handmade card inside, with a drawing of a baby sleeping in a stroller wearing a red cap with yellow zigzags. I recognized the drawing style right away. Maisie's.

Inside there was a message in purple ink:

Dearest Annie—I've knitted you this little cap to keep your ears warm in the cold Toronto winters. All my love, Gran.

Nestled in the tissue paper was a tiny red wool hat with yellow zigzags.

I opened another. The wrapping was covered with little puffins. Inside was another handmade card, this one of a little girl wearing bright green socks.

Dearest Annie—I've knitted you these socks to keep your toes cozy this Christmas.

And in the tissue paper were the bright green socks.

I opened present after present. They all had handmade cards with a picture of a little girl who looked like me wearing whatever the present was: there were sweaters, a couple of scarves, mittens, hats. All with similar notes.

I sat there in the attic, surrounded by a flurry of wrapping paper and knitted things, most too small for me now.

Maisie King was my gran, and she was alive. And for some reason Mom didn't want me to find that out. All she ever told me about her childhood was that her mother had died when she was a little girl and her grandmother brought her up. Then she came to Toronto to university, and her grandmother died before she graduated, and she never went back to Newfoundland.

Mom never wanted to talk about Newfoundland. When I asked her where the painting came from, she said a distant cousin sent it for a wedding present.

My mother lied. She lied about a lot of things.

I thought of my mother taking each present up to the attic, unwrapping it, looking at it, and then wrapping it up again and hiding it away in the trunk. I thought of Maisie, in the living room of Crooked Head Lighthouse, knitting clothes for her unseen grandchild for twelve years. And my mother now, lying in her hospital bed with the curtains pulled shut around her, the green light from the monitors flickering over her face.

I sat there for a long time, trying to figure it out. What was my mother thinking as she hid away those presents? What could have happened that was so bad she never wanted to speak to her mother again? And why did she keep the presents instead of just throwing them away?

And what about my dad? Did he know?

I carefully wrapped each present up again, as best I could, and put them all back in the trunk. Then I went downstairs.

CLAIRE

M Y HEAD HURT. I had the strangest dreams. I was floating in a green tent surrounded by machines that hummed. People were talking to me in a language I didn't understand. There was something I was trying to remember but it kept drifting out of my reach. And my head hurt.

On Monday morning I cornered Mrs. Matchim at recess, after she had led our class through a mind-numbing review of algebra.

"Yes, Claire?" she said, not cracking so much as a smile.

"Can I talk to you for a minute? About next year?"

She glanced at the clock, then motioned to the chair beside her desk. "Certainly. Take a seat."

I sat down and stared at her. No words came.

"Claire?"

"Uh, well, I was wondering if maybe you could help me out with something."

She nodded, waiting.

"It's my mother," I blurted out. "I need help because . . . well, because . . ." I faltered.

Mrs. Matchim frowned. "Is she having second thoughts about you going to high school?"

"No, no, it's not that. It's just . . . just . . . just where I go to high school."

She raised her eyebrows. "Where?"

"I want to go to school in St. John's. To St. Brigid's. I heard it's a good school, and my nan lives there, and I could stay with her and—"

Mrs. Matchim was studying my face. "It certainly has a very good reputation, Claire. It's one of the best high schools in St. John's."

I jumped on this. "Yes, that's one of the reasons I want to go there. I want to get a scholarship so I can go away to Toronto to university."

Mrs. Matchim nodded her head slowly. "Yes, you would have a better chance at St. Brigid's. Better teachers. More students of your caliber to keep you up to the mark. I think it's a wonderful idea."

Phew. So far so good.

"But what was the help you needed, Claire? With your mother?"

"I haven't asked her yet. I was hoping you could talk to her and persuade her it's a really good opportunity for me. She'd listen to you."

Mrs. Matchim frowned again. "I'm happy to discuss this with your mother, Claire, but I think you need to tell her yourself.

It's a family decision. It will be hard for your mother to have you live away."

I shook my head. "No, it's not like that. She doesn't need me around. She's working all the time. But she doesn't understand how important this is to me. She never did well at school so she doesn't get it . . ." I trailed off.

Mrs. Matchim was shaking her head. "Your mother will miss you, Claire, and it's a very big decision to send you away when you're still so young. I do think it would be a good idea, but she may want to wait a year or two—"

"No. I need to go now. I don't want to wait. I—"

The bell for the end of recess rang out. Mrs. Matchim stood up, gathering her books and notes.

"I need to go to my next class, Claire. Once you've told your mother, you can let her know that I support your idea, in theory, and I'll be available to discuss it any time."

I was dismissed. She nodded briskly to me and left the classroom.

So I was still more or less on my own. I'd have to tell Maisie myself.

ANNIE

I LAY DOWN on my bed and stared at the painting. Maisie King. My grandmother. And as of my twelfth birthday,

December 5, just before Christmas last year, still living in Crooked Head, Newfoundland, according to the postmark on the last package. And thinking of me. And knitting me an emerald-green pullover shot with strands of lighter greens, with buttons made of sea-glass. My grandmother.

I never had a grandmother. Or uncles and aunts. Or cousins. It was just Dad, Mom and me. But now there was Maisie. A famous artist. Someone who would understand the way I looked at the world. Someone who saw it the way I did. I closed my eyes.

I must have fallen into a deep sleep. When I opened my eyes, the light had changed. I felt like I had floated up from a long, long way down. I couldn't remember any dreams: only a warm blanket of darkness.

I sat up. I could hear voices downstairs. A woman and a man. Mom? I staggered to the top of the stairs and stopped to listen.

"Do you think we should wake her?" It was Magda, not my mother.

"Certainly," answered my dad.

I walked slowly down the stairs.

"I'm awake," I said, stopping by the kitchen door.

The table was set for two, and Magda had her purse over her shoulder, as if she was about to leave. My father stood leaning against the counter, as if he didn't have the strength to hold himself up anymore. His face was pale.

"There you are," said Magda. "You slept the afternoon away."

"Is Mom—?" I asked Dad. He shook his head.

"No change."

"Come and have your supper, it's all ready," said Magda.

"I'm on my way. I'd stay, but I've got my Italian class tonight." Magda was learning Italian for a trip she was going to take next spring with her sister.

Dad smiled. "That's fine, Magda," he said. "You've been very good to us. We'll be all right on our own now, won't we, Annie?"

I nodded my head and sat down. Magda gave me a kiss, and then left. She'd made us baked chicken breasts coated in crispy bread crumbs, mashed potatoes and corn. Another one of my favorite dinners. I was surprised by how hungry I was. Dad made his way steadily through his full plate, then had seconds.

The book of Newfoundland painters and *Through the Looking-Glass* still sat at the end of the table, where I'd left them this morning. They were where Mom's plate would have been if she was there.

"Dad?" I asked, eyeing the books.

"Mmm?"

"Dad, how come Mom never talks about Newfoundland?"

He shrugged. "No reason. She left there when she was young and never really went back."

"But what about her family?"

"She doesn't have any family. She's told you. Her mother died when she was about twelve and her grandmother brought her up. Then her grandmother died while she was away at university. There was nothing left for her there."

"She was twelve? When her mother died?"

"Yes, I think she was twelve. Twelve or thirteen. It was very sad. She doesn't like to talk about it."

No kidding. Because it didn't happen. "And her name was Morrow, right?"

"Annie," said my father with a sigh, "you know all this. Her maiden name was Morrow and she kept it as a middle name when she married me."

"And she didn't have any sisters or brothers?"

"No. Nobody."

"But that painting in my room, and the quilt—"

"Some distant cousin sent them to us for a wedding present. She told you."

"Then she does have family there."

Dad put down his knife and fork and rested his head in his hands for a moment. Then he looked up at me. I'd never seen him look so tired.

"Look, Annie, I don't know why you're asking all these questions now. But take it from me, your mother has no more family connections in Newfoundland. There was just the one cousin who sent the painting and your mom hasn't been in touch with her for years. Can we drop it now?"

"Sure," I said, and looked away.

Dad didn't know about Maisie. Or Little Annie. Mom had lied to both of us.

CLAIRE

EVERY TIME I looked up from my desk for the rest of the day, all I could see at the window was the blank white fog. When I stepped out of the school at home time I couldn't see farther than about fifteen feet in any direction. The other students pushed past me and went chattering off, some to the bus, some to walk home. I sighed, hoisted my knapsack and trudged along the road.

I went over and over it in my mind. How to tell Maisie. It had to be tonight. I couldn't put it off any longer. There was a knot in my stomach that wasn't going to go away till I got it settled. I walked through the thickening fog, barely noticing anything around me.

When I walked into the kitchen, Maisie was sitting at the kitchen table with an open bottle of wine and a big grin on her face.

"Claire!" she called out happily to me. "I'm so glad you're home. I have some big news for you."

The knot in my stomach tightened and I was immediately on alert.

"Oh?" I said as nonchalantly as I could, putting down my knapsack and peeling off my damp sweater.

"Sit down, we need to talk," said Maisie. Her face was flushed. She didn't usually drink wine in the daytime.

I sat down, trying to ignore the fluttering in my stomach.

"It's wonderful," she said, beaming. "I'm going to have a show in New York. This fall. It's a really big deal, Claire, something I've been wanting for years. I've been planning and Hortense has been negotiating for me and now it's settled. This is a really big breakthrough. And it comes at just the right time, because I really didn't know how I was going to make ends meet this year. Hortense is sure I'll sell lots of paintings there."

Hortense was a gallery owner in St. John's who sold Maisie's paintings and helped publicize her work.

"Well?" said Maisie. "Aren't you going to say anything?"

I looked at her. She hadn't looked that happy in a long, long time.

"It's great, Maisie," I said.

She jumped up and spun around the room. "It's fantastic! New York! Who knows what it could lead to? And we'll be there, Claire, this October for the opening. New York!"

I tried to take it in. New York? We'd actually go there?

Maisie stopped twirling and came over to me.

"There's one thing we need to talk about, Claire," she said, her face solemn. "It's about the work I'm going to be showing." She took my hand and pulled me out of the chair. "Come upstairs."

I let her pull me along, the sense of dread returning. When we got to her studio, she stopped and looked at me.

"This may be difficult for you, Claire, but I think it's time." Then she opened the door and drew me in.

The painting of Annie in her blue pajamas stood on the easel.

"Maisie?" I faltered, turning to her. She put both hands on my shoulders and looked into my face.

"I've been painting Annie, Claire. Ever since she died. And those paintings are going to be in the show."

I just stared at her. Then I began to shake my head.

"No," I whispered, and the room seemed to tilt on one side. "You can't."

"It's time, Claire. We have to move on. This will be good for both of us."

I stepped backward, still shaking my head. "You can't. Everyone will know."

She frowned at me. "Know what?"

I couldn't speak. I stumbled out of the room and down the stairs. I could hear her coming after me but I just kept going. I felt like the house was closing in on me and I couldn't breathe. I burst through the kitchen door and out into the cool, damp fog. Then everything started to tilt again, and I stumbled over something and lost my balance. The road rose up to meet me and I went down hard, banging my head on rock. The world seemed to be spinning out of control and I was lost in the darkness.

PART FIVE

THE
GHOSTS

"I see nobody on the road," said Alice.

"I only wish I had such eyes," the King remarked in a fretful tone. "To be able to see Nobody! And at that distance too! Why, it's as much as I can do to see real people, by this light!"

THROUGH THE LOOKING-GLASS,
AND WHAT ALICE FOUND THERE

ANNIE

A FTER DINNER I helped Dad load the dishwasher, and then I picked up the book of Newfoundland paintings to take it up to my room. Just as I stepped onto the staircase, the phone rang.

Dad picked it up in the kitchen. I waited on the stairs, listening.

"Yes . . . What's happened? . . . and her heart rate? . . . I can be there in fifteen minutes."

A wave of fear washed over me. I heard him hang up the phone.

"Dad?" I whispered.

He came to the door. His face was white. "It's your mom, Annie. She's had a little trouble breathing. I need to go down there."

"Is she . . . ?" I began. "Is she . . . ?"

He came over and put his arm around me. "She's okay. They've put her on a ventilator. But I need to be there."

I looked up at him. "I want to go with you."

He hesitated.

"Please, Dad," I said. "I need to see her."

He nodded. "Okay."

I kept the book of Newfoundland painters clutched to my chest as we drove to the hospital. When we got there, my dad strode ahead and I had to hop a bit to keep up. He nodded to a few people in the hall when we got to the fifth floor, and then stopped outside the ICU.

"Just let me go in for a minute, Annie, and then you can come." He went in, closing the door behind him.

I waited. I could hear voices inside. I felt like I'd been holding my breath since the phone call, that something was frozen inside me and if I let go of it something terrible would happen to Mom.

The door opened behind me.

"Come in, Annie," said Dad. "She's okay."

A nurse brushed by us, giving me a quick smile.

He led me into the ICU and behind the green curtains. Mom was lying very still, just like the last time I saw her, only this time she had a big tube in her mouth that was hooked up to a machine on wheels beside the bed. Her face was very pale.

"That's the ventilator," said my father. "It's helping her breathe. It's all under control, Annie. You can sit with her for a minute. I'm going to talk to her doctor."

I sat down beside the bed and took her hand. The thing

inside me that was stuck moved with a jerk and I felt a burning in my chest.

"Mom," I whispered, "don't leave me. I know about Little Annie and Crooked Head and Maisie. I know all about it. Please don't go."

Then I put my head down on the bed and began to cry.

CLAIRE

I COULD HEAR MAISIE calling me. Slowly the world stopped spinning. My head was pounding.

"Claire! Claire, are you okay?"

I turned over. Maisie was bending over me in the fog.

"Did you hurt yourself?"

I sat up. I still felt sick and my hands were stinging. I shook my head.

She helped me to my feet and we went inside. She got a wet washcloth and held it against my sore hands and the graze on my forehead, just like when I was little and hurt myself.

"Claire, I'm sorry," she said. "I didn't know it would upset you so much."

I stared ahead. I couldn't speak.

"We need to talk about this," said Maisie. "It's time we talked about Annie."

I shook my head.

"Look," said Maisie, sitting beside me. "Annie's gone. We both miss her. We'll always miss her. But we need to move on with our lives. This show will help. I know it will."

"It will help you," I whispered. "It won't help me."

"It will," she said. "It will bring it out in the open."

I shook my head again. "I don't want it out in the open. I don't want people to know."

"But people do know, Claire," said Maisie. "People know about the accident. People know you had a sister who died—"

"People know—" I stopped and swallowed. My throat was aching and each word I said seemed to rip at it. I tried again. "But if we don't talk about it they forget. If you show those paintings, it will all come up again. Everyone will be talking about it. Talking about me."

"The paintings aren't about you, Claire. They're about Annie. No one will be talking about you."

I stood up. "Oh yes they will! Talking about the accident, talking about how I was the one holding her hand, talking about the dog. Maisie, those paintings are all so weird, people will think you're crazy, painting all those pictures of Sammy, making Annie older every year—"

Maisie's eyes narrowed. "Wait a minute. You've seen them?"

"Yes I've bloody seen them!" I shouted. The more words came out, the better my throat felt. "Ever since you started. They're horrible. I hate them."

Maisie was standing up now, her eyes blazing. "You have no right to look at my work. I've told you a hundred times to stay out of my studio."

"I don't care about your stupid work! You spend all your time on that and none on me. Why shouldn't I look at it?"

"You've been spying on me."

"So? How else am I going to know what's going on? Now you're going to take those awful paintings and use Annie and use the accident to make yourself famous, and you don't even care what it will do to me or—"

"Claire, this is how I'm working it out. It's not to make me famous. It's my art. It's how I survive, by painting what I feel."

"But what about what I feel? Don't you even care?"

"Of course I care. I love you."

"Then prove it. Don't show those paintings."

We stood in the kitchen, our eyes locked. Then she shook her head.

"I'm sorry, Claire, I have to show them. It's important to me. And we need the money."

"Then don't ever speak to me again," I said, and walked out of the room.

ANNIE

I LAY WITH MY arm flung over Mom. I could feel her chest rising and falling gently as she breathed. She was warm. I stopped crying after a while, and then in the silence of the room, I could feel her heart beating steadily. And then I could hear my heart, and it seemed like we made a circle, Mom and me. A circle of light.

"Mom?" I whispered. "Claire?" There was no answer. She was far, far away. I heard footsteps behind me and I sat up.

"Annie?"

My father was standing behind me, with a woman in green scrubs.

"This is Dr. Minto," said Dad. "She's going to take a look at your mom."

Dr. Minto smiled at me. She looked tired.

"Maybe you could go to the quiet room to wait," she said, nodding to the nurse who was hovering behind them. I picked up the Newfoundland art book from the end of Mom's bed and went with the nurse.

The quiet room was a few hallways away. It had comfortable chairs, dim lighting, a few magazines on a coffee table. It was empty.

The nurse gave me a quick nod and said, "I'll come back for you when your dad's finished with the doctor." Then she left.

I sat down, hugging the Newfoundland book to my chest.

Everything was very still. Outside this room the life of the hospital hummed.

I closed my eyes. I felt a warmth spreading through me from the book in my arms. Like it was a light, slowly growing stronger. Filling my body with a soft white glow.

Someone came into the room. I opened my eyes. It seemed like the room was filled with light and I couldn't see for a moment. Then my eyes adjusted and I found myself looking up at a little old lady with soft white curls and wire-rimmed spectacles.

"Mrs. Silver? What are you doing here?"

She sat down opposite me and smiled. Today she was wearing a pale-blue dress and a gray cardigan.

"I spend a lot of my time here, Annie. I'm a volunteer. Are you visiting your mother?"

My eyes skittered away from her. "Yes."

"How is she doing?"

"She's . . . um . . . She's having trouble breathing. They had to put her on a ventilator." Mrs. Silver shook her head. "Oh dear. How distressing for you."

I nodded.

Mrs. Silver looked at the Newfoundland book.

"And how's your study of Newfoundland art going, dear?"

"I . . . uh . . . okay."

"I just wondered," she said, drawing some frothy pink knitting out of a big blue bag, peering at it, and then starting to click-clack the needles together as she began to knit. "I just wondered because I had a feeling, the other day in the library, that you were completely transported by the painting you were looking at."

"Trans . . . transported?" I asked.

"Yes, completely. That painting seemed to have a great significance for you."

She looked over her spectacles at me, as if waiting for me to say something.

I didn't know what to say. It seemed like she knew what was happening to me with the paintings, but how could she?

"It's this one artist," I said. "Maisie King."

Mrs. Silver nodded her head. "Your grandmother."

I gasped. "How did you know that?"

Mrs. Silver kept knitting. "Oh, I know a lot of things. About your mother. And her sister. And your grandmother, who still lives at Crooked Head."

"But how—? I don't understand. Are you a friend of my grandmother's?"

"In a way, yes, I am." She put her knitting down in her lap and looked over her spectacles at me again. "Never mind about that now, Annie. What's important is that your mother is in a very bad way and you're the only one who can help her."

I stared at her. "How?" I whispered.

Mrs. Silver nodded at the book. "By going back into the paintings."

CLAIRE

I SAT WRAPPED IN my red blanket, staring out at the fog. My head ached worse than ever. Maisie had left me alone for about an hour, then called me for supper like nothing had happened. When I didn't answer, she came up and stood beside my chair, looking down at me.

"Claire, we need to talk. You need to eat."

I looked into her eyes, then turned away.

"Oh, for goodness' sake," she said, and left the room.

And then I just sat there until the light dimmed and everything went dark.

The next morning, I went down and made my breakfast as usual and went to school, with no sign of Maisie. We were socked in with the fog—Mrs. Matchim said there were onshore winds that were going to keep us in fog and rain for a few days. Then she used that as a jumping-off point to give us a lesson about weather patterns, low air pressure systems, and why the rest of Canada had heat waves in June and we had miserable fog and cold.

When I got home that afternoon, Maisie was waiting for me. I tried to brush by her to go upstairs, but she grabbed my arm.

"Claire, you can't keep this up. We need to talk."

I turned and sat down at the kitchen table, refusing to look at her.

"Claire, you're being childish. I need to have this show. We can talk about how to make it easier for you—"

I examined the scratches on the old table.

"Claire! Will you look at me when I'm talking to you?"

I looked up at her then, my lips firmly clamped shut.

"All right then," she said, getting up. "Be like that. When you decide to act your age, we can discuss it."

I got up and went to my room.

That night, when she called me for supper, I went down. I ate the mashed potatoes, greens and pan-fried cod she put in front of me.

But I never said a word.

I kept it up for three days. Maisie didn't handle it well. After trying to get me to talk a few times, she'd lose her temper and yell, then simmer down and glare at me. She tried ignoring me, but after a while she'd lose patience and start yelling again.

I felt like I had a rock inside my stomach. I didn't know how long I could go on not speaking to her, and I didn't know if it would make her change her mind. But I was so furious with her that I stuck to it. Even though I got lonelier and lonelier, and the silence in the house was as thick and heavy as the fog outside the window.

"Annie," I whispered, sitting in my chair. "Annie, come."

"**Y**ou know," I said. "You know about the paintings."

"Yes," said Mrs. Silver, picking up her knitting again. "And you must go back."

"Then I'm not dreaming," I said. "It's real."

She gave me another look over her spectacles. "You know very well that it's real, Annie. Whether it's a dream or not, it's still real."

I looked at her, knitting away as if this was just an ordinary conversation.

"You left the book for me. At the library. Alice."

She twinkled her eyes at me. "Yes."

"You wanted me to read about the Red King. About his dream."

She laughed. "I knew you'd figure that out. You always were clever."

"My parents don't think so."

"They will. In time."

"So is that what's happening? Mom is like the Red King, dreaming about her life in Crooked Head? And I'm falling into her dreams somehow?"

"Something like that. The important thing is that you keep going there with her. She needs you to see what happened." Mrs. Silver gathered her knitting together and put it into the bag, then stood up.

There was a noise at the door. I looked up. It was the nurse. She gave me a quick, efficient smile.

"Your dad says you can come along now and see your mother."

I scrambled to my feet and turned back to Mrs. Silver.

She was gone.

I looked around. The room was empty. I stuck my head out into the hallway, but it was empty too.

"What are you looking for?" said the nurse briskly.

"That little old lady who was here a minute ago."

The nurse frowned. "I didn't see anyone."

"She was right here. I was talking to her when you came in."

"I don't think so," said the nurse. She seemed to be in a hurry.

I looked around the room. There was a door at the other end.

"Maybe she slipped out this way," I said, crossing the room and opening the door. It led into a different empty hallway.

"Annie?" said the nurse. "Your father is waiting and I need to get back."

I followed her down the hall. "You really didn't see anyone? She was sitting right there opposite me. Knitting."

She glanced at me, her mouth tight. "You were alone when I came in."

Weird.

Dad was sitting beside Mom, holding her hand. He looked up at me.

"There you are," he said, getting up.

"What did the doctor say?" I asked, my eyes on Mom, who looked the same as she had when I left. Pale and still.

Dad looked away. "She's okay. It's a setback, but she's okay for now. We—we can talk about it when we get home. It's late." He walked to the door.

My heart clenched inside my chest. There was something he wasn't telling me.

"Can I say good-bye to Mom?"

He nodded, and left the room.

I went up to the bed and touched Mom's hair. Then I bent over to kiss her forehead. Her skin was soft.

"Hang on, Claire," I whispered. "I'm coming."

CLAIRE

GHOSTS. I DREAMED about ghosts. First there was Annie, smiling at me. Then she disappeared and ghostly shapes drifted past me, gray, filmy, floating ghosts. Flying through the sky around Crooked Head. Like seagulls, or gannets. A flock of ghosts. They didn't mean me any harm. The murmur of their voices and the rustling of their filmy garments were like soft wings fluttering on the breeze from the open window. Ghosts. I drifted away out over the ocean with them, and sleep enfolded me.

Over the years at Crooked Head I thought a lot about ghosts. It started with Ed and the Old Hollies, and then Mary Tizzard and Joan Crocker told me all those stories till I was convinced that the whole headland and the house were maggoty with ghosts. At first every creak in that old house made me jump, and I was always looking over my shoulder, sure there was a ghost nearby. Anytime anyone mentioned a ghost story I would go on alert and listen to every word they said. Kids at school, old-timers I met on the road, people chatting at the general store, friends of Maisie who came to visit. I was drawn to ghost stories like the arrow on a compass is drawn to the north.

I was terrified. Jumpy. Plagued by nightmares. But I still wanted to hear more.

On all those long, long walks home from school that first dreary autumn at the lighthouse, I was sure I would see them. I walked in a bubble of fear, glancing behind me every few feet, scanning the road ahead, always on the lookout. It was scary. But exciting too. I soon discovered that the line between horrifying and delicious is very fine. And slowly my feelings about ghosts began to turn into something else.

I began to look forward to the walks to and from school. I began to anticipate that thrill that would tickle the back of my neck when the road dipped into the woods and the shadows would thicken around me. I welcomed the fog that rolled in across the water, straining my eyes to see a ghost ship gliding toward me. I listened for the whispering of the wind over the grass on the downs, imagining it to be the dead, whispering all around me.

The ghosts became my friends. If this vast emptiness of sky and ocean was populated by the spirits of the dead, then I wasn't alone. And I was closer to Annie.

The third day of not speaking to Maisie, I set off after school through the cottony fog. I knew every step of that walk to the lighthouse so well that I could walk it in the dark, and the fog wasn't as bad as the dark. At least I could see where to put my feet. All I had to do was follow the winding road: up around the hill, down along the causeway, through the trees to the lighthouse. The cool air felt clammy against my face, but I was wearing a thick wool sweater Maisie had knit for me, so I wasn't cold.

I walked slowly. There was nothing to hurry home for. Just Maisie glaring at me and trying to get me to talk.

Foggy days were perfect for ghosts. Everything changed its shape in the fog and took on an air of mystery. A man loomed up at the bend in the road, and then shrunk into a fir tree as I got closer. A dog slunk through the bushes and then solidified into a broken piece of fence. Houses looked like rocks. Rocks looked like houses. And ghosts floated by in streamers of fog.

The causeway was always the scariest place, even when there was no fog, because of the sharp drop on both sides to the beaches below. And because there were just so many ghost stories about those two beaches: a pirate in chains, digging for

135

treasure; a drowned fisherman hauling his boat up on shore; a Newfoundland pony trotting up and down the beach.

I shivered as I began to cross the causeway, imagining the ghosts crawling up the steep sides to grasp at my ankles. The wind picked up and the fog began to swirl around me: one moment it was thick against my face and the next I could see a few feet ahead.

This was where I used to play a game with myself that Annie's ghost would come to me, and she'd be walking beside me as I picked my way along the road, sticking to the middle away from the slippery rocks at the edge. Slipping her warm little hand into mine, the way she used to. And sometimes, sometimes I could almost convince myself that she was there.

"Annie," I whispered. "Come."

ANNIE

I LAY IN THE dark, waiting. Dad sometimes checked on me before he went to bed. I twitched with impatience. I wanted to get to Crooked Head as fast as I could to help Claire.

My bedside clock showed 11:15 in glowing red numbers before I finally heard his footsteps coming heavily up the stairs. Sure enough, he opened my door and walked over to my bed. I lay motionless, pretending to be asleep. He stood there for a moment.

"Good night, Annie," he whispered, and then left. I heard him go into his own room and shut the door.

Poor Dad.

I pulled my flashlight out from under my pillow and took the Newfoundland book from my bedside table. I had to find another picture to fall into.

I flipped through to the Maisie King section. She smiled out at me, her hair white and wild, her eyes alive with humor. I quickly turned the pages, past the painting of the lighthouse in the storm, and stopped at the painting of Annie in the blue pajamas. I stared at it for a minute but nothing happened. There was something weird about the dog on the bed. He didn't look like a friendly stuffed animal. He was kind of scary looking. Something about his eyes. I peered closer. Maisie had painted them as spinning vortexes. I suppressed a shiver and read the caption.

Annie III 1978. Acrylic on canvas. This is the last of the Annie paintings, portraits of a young girl from age 5 to age 8.

The last of the Annie paintings. Did that mean that Maisie stopped painting Annie after that?

These paintings were originally shown in King's breakout show at the Remington Gallery in New York City in 1978. Her first international show, it marked the beginning of her worldwide reputation as one of the twentieth century's finest portraitists. The subject of the paintings was King's daughter, Annie, who was tragically killed when she was four. The portraits reflect how King envisioned her daughter growing older if she had lived. The eerie juxtaposition of the cheerful young girl with the threat of violence gives these portraits the haunting, unsettling tone that is the trademark of King's later work.

Threat of violence? They must be talking about the dog. I glanced at him again. He looked like he was staring at me, ready to pounce. I quickly turned the page.

This painting was very different than anything else I'd seen of Maisie's. At first glance it seemed to be an abstract, with swirling shades of gray. I looked at the caption.

Fog I 1978. Acrylic on canvas. This is the first of King's Fog paintings, a series of four landscapes shown at her second show at the Remington Gallery in New York City in 1979. The paintings became more and more abstract, the first being mostly representational and the last almost completely abstract. The reviews of that show likened her technique to J.M.W. Turner's in his studies of the Thames.

Hmmm. Turner. I looked back at the painting.

It was a subtle mix of gray and white, with some darker shadows. But as I looked closer, the shadows began to take on a recognizable form. A stony road ran along a narrow piece of land, with a steep drop-off on each side to rocky beaches. Halfway across were two small figures, one bigger than the other, walking hand in hand away from the artist. They were walking into a huge gray wall of fog, where indistinct shapes loomed over them. Right at the top of the painting I could make out the outline of a tower with a faint light at the top. The lighthouse?

I peered at the figures. They were children, swathed in bulky sweaters and rubber boots. The fog was swirling round their feet. Gray fingers were pulling at their hair, drawing them into the wall of fog. I could feel the clammy touch of those wisps of fog and I shivered. Then my head began to spin, the room rocked, and I was on my hands and knees on the stony road.

CLAIRE

SUDDENLY I HEARD something scrabbling on the road behind me. I looked up.

I was nearly at the end of the causeway, and the fog ahead of me was a thick gray wall. I spun around. I could just make out a small figure at the far end of the causeway. The fog was closing in fast, licking at the rocks at the edge of the road.

"Hello?" I called out, my mind full of ghosts. Was it really a person? Or just a trick of the fog?

"Hello?" I called out again, my voice cracking. A trickle of moisture ran down the back of my neck. It was starting to rain. The figure seemed to grow bigger and float toward me.

I felt a tremor in my legs and a scream bubbling up. I was within an inch of turning tail and running home as quick as I could when the figure stopped moving.

"Claire?" came a disembodied voice through the fog. "Is that—is that you?"

It was Annie.

I ran to her. Not thinking of the fog, or the uneven road beneath my feet, or the steep drop-offs on both side of the causeway. Not thinking, just running. I swooped her into my arms and gave her a tight hug.

"I knew you'd come back!" I said, laughing. Then I pulled away to look at her.

She was smiling, but there was something odd about her expression. Her eyes were bright, almost as if she was about to start crying. She was dressed in those same blue pajamas with the little flowers on them that she was wearing in Maisie's painting.

"I'm cold," she said, shivering.

I took off my sweater and helped her put it on. It felt just like when she was little and I used to take care of her.

"Come, on, let's get you home out of this fog," I said, taking her hand, and we hurried along the causeway and down the road through the woods.

When we got to the lighthouse, Maisie's truck wasn't there. I got Annie into the kitchen, made two mugs of hot chocolate and gave her the cookie tin to carry.

"Let's go up to my room, so we can hear if Maisie comes home," I said.

"And then I'll hide?" asked Annie, still shivering a bit.

I smiled. "Yes. Under the bed again maybe."

As we settled ourselves on my bed, pulling the quilt over us and opening the tin of cookies, it felt like old times.

"Oatmeal!" said Annie. "My favorite."

"Remember how we used to make them together?" I asked. She nodded and took a big bite.

"Yup."

I smiled at her again. "So you do remember!"

Annie's grin faltered. "I guess I remember some things. I know I always liked making oatmeal cookies with you."

"And drinking cocoa."

"Yes."

"All wrapped up warm in bed."

"Yes." She put the cookie down and her eyes filled with tears.

"Annie," I said, "what's wrong?"

She shook her head, trying to stop the tears that were splashing down her cheeks.

"I just . . . I just miss you."

I put my arm around her shoulders. "You're here now," I said.

I HAD TO GET ahold of myself. I wasn't going to be any use to Mom if I kept dissolving in tears.

She handed me a Kleenex, smiling. Now that I knew Claire was Mom, it was so easy to see it and I wondered why I didn't realize it the first time I saw her. Her face was so much younger, and her skin had no lines, and her features were less sharp, like she was jelly that hadn't quite set yet. But her eyes were exactly the same.

I smiled back and took a sip of the hot chocolate.

"I was hoping you'd come today," she said. "It's been so awful here. Maisie and I are fighting, and this fog won't go away, and everything just keeps getting heavier and heavier, and my head hurts and—"

"Claire," I said, reaching out my hand to her. "It's okay. I'm here. Tell me."

She looked up, her face full of worry. She had that pinched, hungry look I noticed when I first saw her, a look that I recognized now as one I'd seen on my mother's face once in a while. Like she was starving for something she couldn't get and the hunger was tying her up in knots.

"I have to get out of here, Annie. I can't stand living here with Maisie. She never talks to me, and whenever she looks at me, I know she's thinking of the accident and that it was my fault. I want to get away from here, somewhere where no one knows about it, where people won't think of me as the girl who killed her sister—" She began to cry.

I couldn't bear it. I could never stand it when my mother cried. It felt like there were shards of glass inside my chest. "Claire, Claire," I said, putting my arms around her. "You didn't kill her."

"Tell that to Maisie!" she said, her face a mess with tears. "Tell that to all the people who are going to see her paintings of you and Sammy. She's having a show, Annie, in New York, a really big deal, and she's going to be famous as the painter whose daughter died, and everyone will know."

Right. The show.

"I was just about to tell her that I want to go to high school in St. John's in September and she sprang this on me. And now I'm not speaking to her and I don't know what to do."

"High school? In September? But I thought you were the same age as me?"

"I'll be thirteen in October. I should be going into grade eight, but this year I've been doing two years in one."

"They let you do that?"

"Yup. I've got this great teacher, Mrs. Matchim, and she talked Maisie into it. Only Maisie thinks I'll be taking the bus to the high school in Lattice Harbour next year. But I want to go to St. John's and live with Nan and go to school there."

"Will she let you?"

"I don't know! That's what's driving me crazy."

She took a big drink of cocoa and reached for a cookie.

"High school. Wow. You must be . . . pretty smart."

Claire grinned. She looked so much like Mom at that moment that I almost stopped breathing. "I am pretty smart. I can't draw like you and Maisie but I am a brain. I like schoolwork. I love it, actually."

Mom could never understand why I didn't love school the way she did. She loved it so much that she never stopped going. She's a university professor of English and she's never happier than when she's got some old books open on the dining room table and is scribbling away, writing books about books.

"I don't like school," I said, wrinkling my nose. "My mind just wanders off and I start doodling, and then I miss whatever they're talking about. I'm just not that interested. I'd rather draw."

"Just like Maisie," said Claire. "She never did any good at school either. Till she got to art college."

"I might go to an art school," I said. "Next year."

"For grade eight?"

"Yes. My art teacher, Iszák, teaches at this special art school in Toronto. We've been working on getting my parents to let me go. I wanted to go last year but they wouldn't let me. They don't think I should specialize so young. But all I ever want to do is draw. Draw and paint. I know it. And this school is really cool. You take all the regular subjects but you get art every day, and you find the connections all the other subjects have to art. Like, you study art history along with history, and the lives of artists along with English, and you do math along with perspective and all kinds of stuff . . ." I stopped.

It was weird. Here I was chatting away to Claire as if she was my best friend, and she was listening as if she had forgotten for the moment that she thought I was the ghost of her little sister.

"Sounds pretty neat to me," said Claire, and she took one final swig of her cocoa. Then she put her finger in her mug and wiped it to scoop up the dregs of the cocoa that hadn't quite dissolved. Then she stuck her finger in her mouth and sucked it.

Claire. My mother. Doing what she told me a hundred times not to do: sticking her finger in the cocoa mug. I started to laugh.

CLAIRE

FOR SOME REASON Annie was laughing her head off.

"What's so funny?" I said.

"You. Sticking your finger in your cocoa mug," she said. "My mom always tells me not to do that."

"Really? It's the only way to get the chocolatey bits."

"I know!" she said, laughing again and dipping her finger into her own mug.

"So you really live in Toronto?" I asked. "With your mother and father?"

"Yup."

"And it's real? It's not a dream?"

She shook her head. "No. It's real. As real as this."

"That's so weird, Annie. I don't understand how you can be my Annie and have this whole other life."

Her face kind of squidged up as if she was going to start crying again.

"I don't understand either. But I am your Annie. And I want to help you. Only I don't know how."

"Just having you here helps. But I wish you could persuade Maisie not to show the paintings. And to let me go and live with Nan."

Annie frowned. "I don't know if I could persuade her," she said. "I don't even know if Maisie can see me or not. And if she could, I don't know how she would react. Wouldn't she freak out? She'd think I was a ghost."

"She doesn't believe in ghosts. She's always telling me there's no such thing and it's all my imagination."

"Hmmm . . ." said Annie.

"I wonder," I said. We locked eyes. She began to grin.

"Snap!" We both said it at the same time.

"Are you thinking what I'm thinking?" I said.

"Yup," said Annie. "We should haunt her."

"It would be perfect!" I said, scrambling out from under the

146

quilt and grabbing Annie's hands. "You can visit her from beyond the grave and tell her you don't want her to show those paintings to anyone."

"If she can see me that is," said Annie.

"We can work that out. We'll have to experiment."

I jumped out of bed and started pacing around the room. "There are all kinds of ghostly phenomena that people can experience without actually seeing a ghost: sounds, smells, sudden cold. I know them all. I've read so many ghost stories you wouldn't believe. We just have to find a way for you to get your message across."

Annie sat on the bed, her legs crossed, grinning at me. "Won't she suspect something? Like it's you doing it, not a real ghost?"

I shook my head. "Not if we make it really convincing."

"And what if she thinks she's going mad?"

"Well, if she got locked up in a mental hospital then I would have to go and live with Nan."

"I wouldn't feel right about that," said Annie slowly.

"I'm kidding. We just need to find the right balance. Scare her enough not to show the paintings but not enough to push her over the edge. But anyway, Maisie really isn't the type to go off her rocker. She's too practical."

"Then we'll have to work extra hard to convince her that she's being haunted."

"Yes. But we need to start slowly. You can't just jump out in front of her. We'll have to do it scientifically."

I went over to my desk and found an empty notebook and a pen, sat down and began to write. Annie came and stood beside me.

1. Can she see you?
2. Can she hear you?
3. Can she touch you?
4. Can she smell you?

Annie laughed. "Smell? Really?"

"You'd be surprised," I said. "Lots of ghosts bring their own smells with them. There's a story about a fisherman's ghost that was haunting his wife, and she always knew he was nearby because of a strong smell of fish."

"Yes, but wouldn't there often be a smell of fish around?"

"In church? In her bedroom?"

"Oh," said Annie. "Right."

A door slammed downstairs.

"Yikes," I said, jumping up. "That's Maisie. Hide! Under the bed!"

In a flash, Annie was under the bed. That girl could move.

"If she comes in," I whispered, "try making a little noise. Like a knock on the floor. To see if she can hear you."

ANNIE

I T WAS STRANGE to be under the bed again, with the quilt hanging down, just like on the first night. I had a sudden fear that I would be shaken out of the dream again and find myself in my bedroom at home. I didn't know how to stay here.

"Claire?" called Maisie from downstairs.

"I'm up here," answered Claire, and the bedsprings sagged as she sat on the bed.

Footsteps started up the stairs.

One of the empty cocoa mugs appeared in front of my nose, as Claire shoved it under the bed. Hiding the evidence.

"So you're talking to me again, are you?" said Maisie from the door. I winced. Not the most tactful approach.

"I thought maybe if we talked some more you might start seeing things from my point of view," Claire said quietly. One up for Claire.

"I can try," said Maisie. Her footsteps approached the bed and she sat down, but more gently than the last time so I didn't get knocked on the head again. "I see you've been having a snack," she said.

"I was cold when I got home so I made hot chocolate."

"Good. It's miserable out there. Look, Claire, I know you're upset about the Annie paintings. But I'll do everything I can to make it easier for you."

"Everything except not show them."

"I told you. That isn't an option. Think of it this way: it's going to be in New York, not St. John's, and I'll make sure the publicity says as little as possible about the accident. The fact that you were there doesn't even need to come up."

"That's not the point. I don't think Annie would want those paintings to be seen. They're so creepy."

"I know they're creepy. That's what makes them good."

"But it's Annie you're painting, Maisie! It's like you're using her and what happened to her for your own benefit. It's not fair. She wouldn't like it."

"I don't think we can start to speculate about what Annie would or wouldn't like, Claire. This is my art. And we have to eat. If I don't do the show, I'll be completely broke by Christmas. I know it's difficult for you, but you're going to have to come to terms with it."

Right. Time for Annie to have her say. I knocked on the floor three times. "What was that?" said Maisie.

Bingo! She could hear me!

"What was what?" said Claire innocently.

"That knocking. There must be someone at the door. Who on earth? In this fog?"

Maisie got up and I heard her footsteps going downstairs.

The quilt that was hanging down over the side of the bed flipped up and Claire's head appeared upside down, grinning at me.

"That was great, Annie," she whispered gleefully. "Keep it up!" and then she whisked her head away and the quilt fell back into place as Maisie's footsteps returned up the stairs.

"That's funny," said Maisie. "There was no one there."

"Maybe it was the wind," said Claire.

"Maybe," said Maisie. "Now, where were we?"

"I was saying that I don't think Annie would want you to show those pictures. Have you even thought about that? It's like the whole world will know what happened to her and think of her as that poor girl in those weird pictures."

"I'm trying to show what she was like, Claire; it's a tribute to her. It's not taking anything away from her memory."

"Do you think she'd want the world to know that she ran across the street after some stupid dog and that's why she died? That's what those pictures all say. Annie wouldn't like it."

"Claire, this is ridiculous. Annie is dead. Nothing we do now is going to hurt her."

"But it hurts me! Can't you see that?"

"I don't understand, Claire. It just doesn't make sense. The show will be in New York, and you don't even have to go if you don't want to. You can stay here and it doesn't need to touch you at all."

"It does touch me. And it touches Annie. She wouldn't like it; I know she wouldn't."

My cue. I knocked on the floor again: three loud knocks.

"There it is again!" said Maisie. "You must have heard it that time."

"I didn't hear anything," said Claire.

I had to bite my thumb not to start laughing. She sounded so innocent.

Maisie heaved herself off the bed and went stomping downstairs to investigate. I reached out to push the quilt aside so I could talk to Claire, but as I touched it, I felt that tilting feeling again. I thought for a second that I could feel Claire's hand, but then it got really dark and I was lying on my own bed, holding tight to my quilt, with the Newfoundland book lying open beside me, just visible in the dim light filtering in my curtains from the streetlight outside my window.

CLAIRE

I REACHED DOWN TO push the quilt aside and talk to Annie. I touched her hand and then it slipped away. I stuck my head down to look but she was gone. There was nothing but dust under the bed.

Maisie was muttering to herself downstairs. I could hear her opening and closing the kitchen doors and then going down the hall to the check the other door. I laughed softly. We'd made a good start.

PART SIX

THE HAUNTING

And I wish you wouldn't keep appearing and
vanishing so suddenly: you make one quite giddy.

Alice, ALICE'S ADVENTURES IN WONDERLAND

ANNIE

M Y FLASHLIGHT WAS lying on the floor. The batteries were dead. I switched on the light beside my bed and looked at my clock. Three-fifteen.

The house was quiet. I picked up the Newfoundland book and looked at the fog picture. Funny. It said that Maisie painted it in 1978, the same year she painted the picture of Annie in my blue pajamas. But why were there two girls? One big, one smaller. Claire and Annie. If Maisie didn't believe in ghosts, what was she painting? What she wanted to see? I wondered if she'd painted other pictures of Annie over the years.

I stared at the fog painting for a minute or two, trying to will myself into it. But nothing happened. Maybe it only worked once with each painting?

I turned the page.

Ida Doyle 1984. Acrylic on canvas. One of King's innovative Portraits of a Landscape series where she paired portraits with landscapes. The companion painting (opposite) expresses the inner landscape of the subject.

The painting was of an older woman with graying hair pulled back from her weather-beaten face. Her eyes were tired and sad, and she wore an apron. On the opposite page was a painting of the ruins of a wharf out over the rocks in a small cove. Interesting. The two paintings were connected by color and tone. It was as if I was looking inside the woman's life and experiencing her innermost heart, which took the form of this abandoned site.

I jerked up. I'd been staring at these paintings for a couple of minutes and there was no sign of me going into them. They didn't seem to have any connection with Claire. I turned through the next few pages, but all the paintings were from later years, and although they were vivid and compelling, and I longed to linger over them, none of them brought me back to Crooked Head.

I had to find more of Maisie's paintings.

CLAIRE

I WENT DOWNSTAIRS TO find Maisie standing at the front door, looking out into the rain. The wind had picked up and the fog was starting to lift.

"Did you find out what was making the knocking sound?" I asked.

She shook her head. "There's no one here."

"There's lots of ghost stories with mysterious knocking. Sometimes it's Death, calling to carry away a dead person's soul."

"Oh, for goodness' sake, Claire," said Maisie, shutting the door with a slam and going into the kitchen.

"Or sometimes it's a spirit trying to communicate with the living," I said, following her. Maisie began unpacking the groceries.

"And I suppose the next thing you're going to say is that it was Annie, come to tell me not to put the paintings of her in my show!"

"I didn't say that. How many knocks were there?"

Maisie took a loaf of bread out of her shopping bag and put it on the kitchen table. "Three. Both times there were three sharp knocks."

"Oh dear," I said.

She turned on me. "What do you mean, oh dear?"

"When things come in threes in ghost stories that's always a bad sign."

She started loading tins of soup and tuna fish and condensed milk into cupboards.

"I'm sure there's a simple explanation. This old house has lots of strange noises."

"But they don't usually come in threes."

"Claire, if you're playing some silly trick on me, you can just stop it. I'm not going to be spooked out of showing the paintings. This is just childish."

"I'm not saying anything, Maisie. You were the one who heard the knocking. I didn't. And you were sitting right beside me so you know it wasn't me."

"It's all nonsense, Claire. I'm sorry you're upset about the show but it's going to happen. And there's something else I want to talk to you about."

"What?"

"I ran into Mrs. Matchim at the store and she asked me if we'd been discussing your plans for next year. I assumed she was talking about you going to the high school in Lattice Harbour, but when I brought it up, she got all evasive and said I should ask you. What's that all about?"

Oh great. Now I had to tell her. I took a deep breath.

"I was talking to Mrs. Matchim about . . . about . . . about this idea I had for school."

"What idea? Don't you want to go to high school after all? I wondered if you were ready. I mean, it's a big change—"

"No, it's not that. I want to go ahead. But . . . but . . ."

Her eyes were fixed on me. I felt everything go tight in my chest. I took another deep breath and just said it.

"But I want to go in St. John's. I want to go to St. Brigid's and live with Nan."

"What?" Maisie's eyes kind of popped. "You're kidding, right?"

"No. It's a good school. Way better than the one in Lattice Harbour. I'll get a proper education there, and the teachers are really good, and some of my old friends go there, and I'll have a better chance of getting a scholarship for university—"

"University?" said Maisie. "You're not even thirteen yet. You don't need to worry about university."

"I need to plan ahead," I said, and I crossed my arms over my chest and glared at her.

"And you want to leave Crooked Head?"

I nodded.

"And live with Nan?"

I nodded again.

"Over my dead body," she snapped, and stormed out of the room.

ANNIE

AT BREAKFAST THE next morning I was bleary-eyed. The air felt thick, like the fog in Crooked Head, and it was a big effort to move my arm to pick up my toast. Sitting across from me, Dad didn't look much better. He had woken me up at seven o'clock, saying that it would be a good idea for me to go back to school today. Magda wouldn't be able to come till the afternoon, and he had to go to the hospital.

It was one of those hot June mornings when the sun starts to bake the pavement as soon as it rises. I was wearing my green shorts with a white tank top and my sandals: the coolest clothes I could find. As I stood at the door with my knapsack on my back, about to leave for school, I stopped for a moment, looking out at our quiet, tree-lined street. Then I turned back to Dad, who was putting on his jacket and checking for his car keys.

I gathered my courage as best I could. "Dad?" I said. He looked up.

"About Mom." My voice came out in a little squeak. I cleared my throat. "What does it mean that she's on the ventilator now? Does it mean she's getting worse?"

He sighed and came and put his hand on my shoulder. "It's not a good sign, Annie. I don't want you to worry though. Sometimes these cases are very unpredictable. She could be breathing on her own again in a day or two. They just can't find any reason for it. It's puzzling."

"So she could still . . . she could still wake up?"

"Oh yes. There's a very good chance she will. We just have to be patient." He sounded a bit too hearty to me. Like he didn't really believe it.

He gave my shoulder a squeeze. "You go on to school now, Annie. Magda will be here when you get home. And I'll call the school if there's any change."

I nodded and set off. When I got to Queen Street I stopped. If I turned right and walked about five blocks, I'd be at school. If I turned left and walked two blocks, I'd be at the library.

I turned left.

I had to skulk in the park for about half an hour before the library opened. I sat on a bench under a tree, staring blindly at some bright-red flowers in a formal flower bed. People were walking dogs and pushing strollers. I was hoping that the school would think I was still staying home because of Mom's accident and wouldn't start phoning Dad to see where I was. I needed to find more of Maisie's paintings and get back to Crooked Head.

I was the first person through the door when one of the librarians unlocked it. I went right to the art section where I'd found the Newfoundland book. There were no more books of Newfoundland art there, and when I looked under *K* for King, there was nothing. I went to the desk where the computer was and looked it up in the catalogue.

Under Maisie King there was one book: *Maisie King: A Retrospective.* It had "Reference Library" listed beside it.

I knew where the Reference Library was: right downtown. It wasn't that far from where I went for art lessons. Occasionally Mom and I would go there together on Saturdays after my class.

She'd leave me in the art section looking at books of paintings while she wandered off to look at displays of rare books or do a bit of research. Mom loved libraries.

I could find my way there on the streetcar and the subway. Easy. As I left the library, I took a quick look around to see if Mrs. Silver was there. She said she came nearly every day. There was no sign of her. Maybe she was volunteering at the hospital today.

It was rush hour and the streetcar was packed. But I wiggled on and struggled through to the back, where there was always a seat. Mom taught me that. We usually went by transit to my art class because it was hard to park downtown. She'd go off and do errands, or go to the library until it was time to pick me up.

I couldn't stop thinking of Mom. Everywhere I went there was something to remind me of her. How did she get from that unhappy girl at Crooked Head, Newfoundland, to become Professor Jarvis at Glendon College in Toronto? She never told me much about her life before university, meeting Dad and having me. One way or another, I was going to find out what happened. And bring her back.

I closed my eyes and I could see her lying in her bed in the hospital, with her white face and the tube in her mouth. I remembered how it felt when our hearts beat together making a circle of light around us.

"Hold on, Claire," I said silently. "I'm coming."

CLAIRE

CROOKED HEAD WAS too small to have a library. We had a Bookmobile. It was a bus fitted up like a library, with shelves full of books and a checkout desk. The Bookmobile came every three weeks and parked in the school parking lot for a few hours. Two sisters, May and June Teasel, drove it around from community to community, up and down all kinds of bad roads and awkward hills, from Conception Bay to Trepassey. It took them three weeks to make the circuit, then they'd start again.

I don't know what I would have done without that Bookmobile. Every three weeks I was there returning books and getting more. At first I was only allowed four books at a time, but once I made friends with the Teasels, and they realized what a fast reader I was, they let me take out eight. I read Dickens, Mark Twain, Kipling, Wodehouse. And of course, all of L.M. Montgomery's books, E. Nesbit, Arthur Ransome, Mary Stewart, Daphne du Maurier. Edgar Allan Poe and whatever ghost stories they could find for me. Nancy Drew and Philomena Faraday, and countless others. I never felt better than when I walked home from school with my eight new books weighing down my knapsack, with all that new reading ahead of me.

The day after Maisie put her foot down about me going to St. John's was a Bookmobile day. I went out at lunchtime and handed in my books, then headed toward the back of the bus where there was a very small section on the supernatural. I had one particular book in mind, and luckily, it was there.

Are You Being Haunted? by Philomena Faraday. It was a slim little book, a companion to her novels. The Teasels did their best to order in books that I asked for. Faraday had a ghost series of about fifteen books, and I'd read most of them. As well as writing fiction, she was a student of ghost lore, and this book listed all the ways you could tell if you were being haunted.

I picked some other books and checked them out. Usually I would stop and have a little chat with the Teasels, about books and reading, but today my heart wasn't in it. I mumbled something to them and went back into school.

When I was accelerated into grade eight, I was allowed to stay in the classroom after lunch to work on catching up with the rest of the class. Mrs. Matchim would often come in and do some work at her desk while I was there.

Today I sat flipping through the Faraday book, trying to concentrate on finding some hints about how to haunt Maisie, but I couldn't focus.

Maisie had turned the tables and now she was giving me the cold shoulder. She had stayed in her studio for hours the night before, and I finally made myself a fried egg and toast for supper. Then I went to bed. I felt like I had hit a roadblock and I didn't know what to do next. When Annie came back, we could carry on with haunting Maisie so she wouldn't show the paintings, but even if that worked, how was I going to persuade her to let me move to St. John's? Especially when she wasn't talking to me.

"Claire?"

Mrs. Matchim was sitting at her desk, looking at me. I hadn't even heard her come in.

"Are you all right?"

I guess I had been staring off into space. "Yes. I'm just—" I didn't know what to say.

She got up and came to sit in the desk beside me. "I saw your mother in the store yesterday and I think I may have put my foot in it. I thought you would have discussed your plans with her by now."

I shook my head. "No. But we did last night."

I fell silent again.

"And?"

"And she said no. She doesn't want me to go."

Mrs. Matchim sighed. "I thought that might happen. It would be hard for your mother to be without you."

"But she doesn't pay any attention to me when I'm there!" I protested. "I don't see why it's such a big deal. She could come in to St. John's on weekends."

"You're her only child," said Mrs. Matchim. "Mothers want to be with their children. They can't just let them go. Especially when they're so young. When I was sixteen and left home to go to college, it nearly broke my mother's heart. And I was older than you."

I looked at her. Hard to imagine Mrs. Matchim ever being sixteen. Or having a mother.

"Would you talk to her? Tell her how important it is for me?"

"I can talk to her but I'm not sure how far I'll get. If she's decided that she doesn't want you to go, I doubt if I'll change her mind."

"At least she'll see it's not just me, that another grown-up thinks it's a good idea."

"What about your grandmother? Could she talk to her?"

I shook my head. "Nan won't go against Maisie. She never does. Maisie always gets what she wants."

Mrs. Matchim stood up. "You can tell her to come in and talk to me tomorrow after school. I'll do my best, Claire, but it really is your mother's decision."

Right. And Maisie had already made it. She didn't want me going.

As I walked home that afternoon I mulled it over. What could I do to get her to let me go?

Something so awful she wouldn't want me around anymore. Something that would make her want to get rid of me.

ANNIE

THE METRO LIBRARY was busy, with a steady stream of people loaded down with knapsacks passing through the turnstiles. I crowded into the little elevator to go to the fifth floor. It was all glass on one side, and it zoomed up from floor to floor. The whole center of the building was empty space, circled by white walls for each floor. The empty space got bigger and the floor space got smaller with each floor. I could see people sitting at tables, working or wandering through the aisles of books.

The fifth floor had the art section in one corner, overlooking a park. I went to a computer and looked up the online catalogue. I wrote the call number on a slip of scrap paper, found the right aisle and followed the numbers till I got to the *K*s.

There it was. *Maisie King: A Retrospective*. I lifted it down. It was big and heavy. I glanced at the front cover. It was a stunning Newfoundland landscape with cliffs and water. I quickly looked away. I didn't want any accidents.

There were a few big armchairs placed in front of the floor-to-ceiling windows. I chose one all by itself in a corner, then settled into the chair with the book on my lap. I closed my eyes for a moment. The book seemed to radiate heat. This was it. My way back to Claire.

I wanted to go right away. But I had to be careful which painting I chose. And I wanted to find out more about Maisie.

I opened my eyes. I could see the tops of the trees in the park, green leaves fluttering. A few birds darted to and fro.

I opened the book without looking at the cover and went right to the index.

"Annie" was right there under *A*, listing her portraits, *Annie I, Annie II* and *Annie III*. No *Annie IV*. I scanned down to the *C*s. No Claire. I looked under the *K*s. Annie and Maisie were there, and Alexander King and Ellen King, who must be Maisie's parents. But no Claire.

What happened? Didn't Maisie paint Claire? Shouldn't she be mentioned, somewhere?

I turned to the introduction and scanned it. It talked more about Maisie's paintings than her life, with only a passing mention of her parents and the bald statement, "Her daughter Annie died at the age of four. The Annie series is a tribute to her."

It was like Claire never existed.

I started turning the pages, covering each painting with a piece of paper torn out of a school notebook, and reading the captions first. I wanted to choose which painting to go into.

All the paintings from the other book were there, and after the *Fog I* painting came one called *Empty*.

Empty 1978. Acrylic on canvas. This is an excellent example of King's ability to establish a mood. The cozy chair by the window and the crumpled red blanket are in stark contrast to the endless horizon of the sea.

Red blanket? That sounded familiar. I snuck a look under the paper.

It was Claire's room, with her big chair in front of the window. The red blanket that was wrapped around her the first night I saw her lay tumbled half on the chair and half on the floor.

A tidy desk stood in the corner, and I could just see the corner of her iron bed frame with the blue-and-white quilt hanging down. The sunlight coming in the window cast a dappled pattern on the floorboards, overlaid with the elongated shadow from the window panes.

I looked a little closer to see how she got that effect, and then the shadow started to shimmer and the Metro Library tilted way up into the sky and I was falling through the window, through the tops of the trees and tumbling down onto the bare wood boards of Claire's room at Crooked Head.

CLAIRE

WHEN I GOT home from school, Maisie wasn't there. I went straight up to her studio and tried the door. It was locked. I guess she didn't want me spying on her anymore.

I ducked into the closet in the hall and made my way through to the door into the Piercey side of the house. I went into the middle room and started looking for the Annie paintings.

I went through all the canvases in the room. The Annie paintings were gone. Maisie must have moved them into the studio. I sat on the bed and gazed blindly out the window.

She didn't trust me with them. She was going to keep them locked in the studio until she sent them away for the show. And I wouldn't get to look at them again.

Even though I thought they were creepy, I'd been sneaking into the Piercey side of the lighthouse to look at the Annie paintings every few weeks.

They made me feel horrible. But I had to look at them. To see Annie again. Because whatever else I thought about Maisie and her art, she had somehow captured Annie's spirit in those paintings. We learned in school that people used to be superstitious about taking photographs because they thought that the pictures robbed them of their souls. That's what Maisie's paintings of Annie were like. She had the very essence of Annie there in that paint on that canvas, like a butterfly pinned to a card.

Sitting in the cold, deserted side of the house looking at all those paintings of Annie, I felt like I was with her again. Even though it hurt to look at them, like I had a fishhook stuck down my throat. When I looked at those paintings, everything I felt about her death came rushing back and it was almost too much to bear. Annie's spirit shone out—her playful, joyful spirit—but Sammy was always there. The gruesome black dog that led her to her death. And Annie's impulsive I-don't-care-about-anything-but-what-I-want attitude was there too, the thing in her that made her always get the biggest piece of chocolate cake, the thing that made her suck all the attention in the room to her, the thing that made her forget all the warnings about cars and run across the street to Sammy. Maisie saw it and she painted it into those pictures. And they made me feel awful.

Because I hated that part of Annie. I hated it when she was alive because it helped push me into the background. Nobody ever saw me when Annie was in the room, including Maisie and Nan. And then when she died, she still drew all the attention away from me. Because her death hung in the air between Maisie and me wherever we went. And it always would.

But I didn't want the world to see any of that. Because then they'd all blame me even more for her death. They'd say I wanted her dead. I could see it now: all the fashionable people in the New York gallery standing in front of the Annie paintings and speculating about how she died.

"An accident?"

"Yes, she got hit by a car, running after that little black dog."

"Oh, isn't that dreadful! Poor little thing. What was she doing out on the street by herself?"

"Apparently her older sister was with her, but she wasn't paying attention and let go of her hand."

"Some people said the sister was jealous, because the little one got all the attention, and that's why she was so careless."

"You mean she did it on purpose? But that's . . ."

"Murder, yes, she murdered her little sister."

I stood up quickly to make it stop, and the voices faded into the screeching of seagulls outside the window. I looked out over the blue sea. The fog had lifted today and it was almost warm, except for a cool breeze from the east.

It was true, I was angry with Annie that day. I was furious. But I didn't want her to die. And now, now that she had come back to me, I wasn't angry at all. It seemed like all that selfishness had gone out of her. Also a lot of her spirit. She seemed a paler reflection of the Annie I knew. She wasn't what I expected Annie to be like when she got to be my age. And she said she came from Toronto and had a life there.

A picture came into my mind. A picture of Annie, in a kitchen, sitting at a table drawing a salt and pepper shaker. I was cooking and I turned around and she smiled up at me. Then it dissolved.

I gave my head a little shake. I still had the remnants of headache that had been bothering me for days. I couldn't think about where Annie came from or what kind of life she had now. I knew she was my Annie, and that was enough.

I had to get into Maisie's studio. I scooted back through the cupboard and into Maisie's room and started searching for the key. Maisie's room was in its usual state of complete disorder, with her clothes piled up on a chair and the floor, her dresser a jumble of necklaces and scarves. I started at the bedside table.

There was a photograph of Annie in a pewter frame sitting beside her clock. Maisie had kept it by her bed ever since Annie died. It was taken that last summer, in our backyard in St. John's, with Annie grinning up at the camera, a lilac bush in full bloom behind her. It caught at my heart, the way photos of Annie always did.

Suddenly there was a banging noise in my room next door, like the sound of someone tripping and falling. The photo slipped out of my hands, but I caught it before it crashed to the floor. I froze. Maisie? Home? In my room? I glanced out the window. No sign of the truck. Not Maisie then.

I tiptoed silently down the hall and peeked around the door-frame into my room. Annie was sitting on the floor with a dazed look in her eyes.

ANNIE

"ANNIE!" CRIED CLAIRE, running over to me and giving me a fierce hug. "You came back!"

"It's getting harder each time," I said, rubbing my knees. "More like falling."

"Falling?"

"Yes. This time it was like falling off the roof of a building. I was in the library, and it felt like the whole building was turning upside down—"

Claire rubbed her forehead, as if she had a headache. "Well, never mind that. You're here now. There've been some new developments." She started rooting through her knapsack.

I stood up and went over to the chair and lightly touched the red blanket, which was hanging over the side, just like in the picture. I wondered when Maisie painted it. And why.

Claire came over and stood beside me.

"Where's Maisie?" I asked.

"Out somewhere. She's mad at me. She found out about me wanting to go to St. John's for high school and she said no."

"Really? But that's what you end up—I mean . . ." I stopped myself. "I . . . uh . . . I thought she'd say yes."

"'Over my dead body' were her exact words. So now we have to figure out a way to get her to say yes, as well as stopping her from showing the Annie paintings."

"Wow. How are we going to do that?"

"I don't know. I got this book about haunting at the Bookmobile today. It might give us some ideas."

I sat down in the big chair. "Let's have a look."

Claire squeezed in beside me.

"A big chair for two to curl up in," I murmured, without thinking, and Claire started to laugh.

"You remember!"

"I . . . uh . . ."

"That's what we always used to say when we sat together in a big chair. From *The Friendly Giant*. Your favorite TV show."

And that was always what Mom said to me when I was small and we curled up together in a big chair. She told me about watching a TV show called *The Friendly Giant* when she was little. But I'd never seen it. It was one of the only things she ever told me about her childhood.

"One little chair for one of you and a bigger chair for two more to curl up in; for someone who likes to rock, a rocking chair," said Claire and I together, and then we both started laughing.

"It's just like old times, Annie," said Claire happily.

"Yup," I said. It was. But not the way she thought. I couldn't tell her. I couldn't break the spell. I had to just keep playing along and hope that somehow this was all going to work out and I'd have my mother back.

"So," said Claire, starting to turn the pages of the book. "What have we got here? Mysterious knocking. We've done that. Cold spots. Don't know how we'd manage that."

"What are cold spots?" I asked. She was looking at a badly drawn picture of a man looking scared and surrounded by icicles. It looked like a pretty cheesy book.

"It's really scary," said Claire, who didn't seem to notice how silly the book was. "It happens in a lot of ghost stories. A cold spot will suddenly form in your house, where there's the presence of a ghost. It's like they suck all the warmth out of the space they occupy." She frowned and glanced at me for a moment, then turned back to the book.

"I don't think we could fake that," I said doubtfully.

"No," she said, flipping through the book. "Footsteps. Laughing. Singing. Someone calling your name."

"We could do some of those. I could do the footsteps, maybe when she's downstairs."

"And we could experiment to see if she can hear you. Or see you."

We looked at each other for a moment.

"That's the big one," I said softly.

"Yes," said Claire slowly. "If she can see you, then you should be able to change her mind. But we have to do it carefully. We don't want to push her too far. Maisie is so dramatic. She might do something rash."

"Like—?"

Claire frowned. "I'm not sure. I just never know what to expect from Maisie. She might go a bit crazy. Or decide that this is a great opportunity to paint another portrait of you as a ghost."

I laughed.

Claire didn't.

CLAIRE

I STARTED FLIPPING through the book again.

"Objects being out of place," I read out. "Doors opening and closing. There are all kinds of ideas here. We could do it, Annie. And maybe I'll leave this book somewhere she'll notice it, like in the bathroom."

"What happened the other night after I did the knocking? Did she think it was a ghost?"

I smiled. "She was freaked. She couldn't figure it out. And I kept saying I didn't hear anything, but I pointed out that mysterious knocking is a sure sign of a ghostly visitation." Annie grinned. "I think it will work. We just have to take it slow."

The door downstairs slammed. We both jumped.

"She's back!" I said.

"Okay," said Annie, with that wicked gleam in her eyes I knew so well. "Let's start with some ghostly footsteps."

I gave her arm a squeeze then headed downstairs.

Maisie was in the kitchen, pulling things out of the fridge to start supper.

"Maisie?" I said.

She turned and gave me a dirty look. "What?"

"Are you still mad at me?"

She gave a big, theatrical sigh and dumped some carrots and cabbage on the table. "I'm not *mad* at you, Claire, I'm just disappointed."

"And by 'disappointed' you mean mad, right?"

"No," she replied, taking a big knife and starting to chop the cabbage. "I mean disappointed. I'm disappointed that you talked this over with Mrs. Matchim without even mentioning it to me. And I'm disappointed that you feel you would be better off living with Nan in St. John's than you are here with me."

"It's not about you, Maisie. It's about me getting a better education."

"You could do perfectly well at the high school in Lattice Harbour. You don't need to be taking Latin and Greek and all that foolishness."

"I do! I want to go to university and study English. I need all kinds of things I can't get at Lattice Harbour and I can get at St. Brigid's. You shouldn't hold me back just because you don't like the same things I do. What if Nan had told you that you couldn't go to art school when you were young? How would you feel?"

"It's not the same, Claire," said Maisie, taking a carrot and starting to hack at it. "You're going into grade nine, not university. There will be time for all that later."

"I want it now. I don't want to be stuck here and bored out of my head for the next three years. There's nothing for me in Crooked Head."

"Well, we're not moving back to St. John's. And you're staying here with me whether you like it or not."

Upstairs, a door slammed. Maisie gave a start. "The wind must be picking up. Can you go close the windows upstairs?"

I didn't move.

"Claire? Don't start sulking. Just do what I asked."

Before I could move there was the clear sound of footsteps walking along the hall upstairs.

"Who's that?" said Maisie. "Have you got a friend here?"

I glared at her. "I don't have any friends, remember?"

"Well, who is it then?"

"Who is what? I didn't hear anything."

Maisie stopped chopping the vegetables and put her hands on her hips. "Claire, stop fooling around. Who is here? I heard footsteps."

"There's nobody here, Maisie. I didn't hear footsteps."

A door slammed again. "You heard that!"

"What?"

"Claire, I'm not in the mood for your nonsense." She charged out the door and up the stairs.

ANNIE

I DUCKED INTO THE hall closet just as Maisie burst out of the kitchen door. I stood motionless, holding my breath, even though I could feel a giggle building up inside me.

I could hear her banging around, opening doors and muttering to herself. Then Claire's voice, floating up the stairs, as she followed her mother up.

"I told you there was no one here, Maisie. You must be hearing things."

"I am not hearing things," said Maisie, right outside the closet door. "There were footsteps."

Before I could move, she opened the door and stood looking in, right at me.

Maisie was taller than I thought she would be, with thick brown hair curling over her shoulders. Her eyes were the same blueberry-blue as Claire's—and they looked right through me. I didn't dare move a muscle. She shivered.

"There's definitely a draft coming through here," she said over her shoulder to Claire. "It's freezing." I pressed myself up against the wall as she came in. Maisie brushed by me and headed along to the door at the far end. Claire followed, making a funny face at me as she passed. I stayed in the corner. It felt weird to be invisible. Really weird. Like I could easily float away into nothing. I bit down on my thumb till it hurt. That made me feel more solid.

I could hear Maisie striding through the Mirror House, apparently looking in every room and every cupboard. "Well, that's the strangest thing," she said, as she ducked back into the closet and came toward me. "Not a window open. I wonder—" Then she stopped, right beside me. "It's very cold, right here," she said, shivering. Claire came up behind her. "Can you feel that, Claire? Like ice. There must be some air getting in from somewhere."

"It doesn't feel any different to me, Maisie," said Claire. "And it's warm outside. There's no wind and the sun is shining."

Maisie walked out into the hall and peered out the window.

"You're right," she muttered, then walked back into the closet, standing so close to me I could feel her breath. "But it's freezing in here. Just in this one spot."

"There is an explanation," said Claire. "But you're not going to like it."

Maisie whirled around and shook her finger at Claire. "Don't start with me again about ghosts, Claire. I'm going to finish supper." She stalked down the stairs.

Claire came into the closet and silently closed the door behind her.

"How did you do that, Annie?" she whispered. "How did you make it cold?"

I shrugged. "I don't know. Do you feel cold around me?"

She shook her head. "Never. If anything, I feel warm," and then she gave me a big hug.

She felt warm to me too. I closed my eyes. She smelled just like Mom. Lavender soap. Then the floor in the closet tipped up and I was slipping down and then I was falling and falling, a long way down, through darkness, by myself. Claire was gone.

CLAIRE

ONE MINUTE I was hugging her and the next my arms were closed on nothing. Annie was gone.

I leaned my head up against the wall and shut my eyes. There was a dull kind of throbbing in my head. I wished Annie would just stay, and not keep coming and going.

"Claire!" Maisie's voice echoed up the stairs "Can you come and give me a hand with dinner?"

"I'll be right there," I called back, going into my bedroom and getting the *Are You Being Haunted?* book from the chair where I left it. I tiptoed into Maisie's bedroom and left the book on her bedside table, strategically placed just in front of the photograph of Annie. Then I went down to supper.

We had a quiet dinner. Maisie didn't bring up the subjects of footsteps, cold spots or high school in St. John's. Instead she started in on a long monologue about how she and Ed were going to fix up one of the sheds so she could keep chickens.

I tuned her out. I was trying to figure out how I could steal her keys and get into the studio. She usually kept her car keys and house keys in the pocket of her jacket. If she had put the studio key on that ring, I would have to steal them when she was asleep. Otherwise she would catch me.

That night I set my alarm for five o'clock the next morning. Maisie was dead to the world till at least nine o'clock, so I would have lots of time to get into the studio and look at the Annie paintings. I went to sleep and had a strange dream. I was sitting in a rocking chair holding a baby and rocking back and forth. The baby was sleeping. I was in a city, and there was the noise of cars outside the window. Sun streamed in. The baby woke up and looked at me, and smiled.

It was Annie.

ANNIE

I OPENED MY EYES. I was in my quiet corner of the library and there was no one else around. The book, open to the painting of Claire's room, still lay on my lap.

I had to get back to Crooked Head. I stared at the painting for a couple of minutes, but nothing happened. I turned the page.

Little Annie grinned out at me. She was standing in front of a city house with a black Scottie dog in her arms. It was the first painting Maisie did of Little Annie after she died. She was about five, bursting with life, laughing.

"Annie," I whispered. "Can you take me to Crooked Head? Can you take me to Claire?"

Nothing happened. I tore my eyes away from hers and read the caption.

Annie I 1975. Acrylic on canvas. This is the first of the Annie series, based on King's vision of how her daughter Annie would have grown up, if her life hadn't been cut short by a terrible car accident when she was four. King never speaks about her daughter but lets her paintings tell the story of her great loss.

I glanced back at the painting. Funny how the black dog drew my eye away from all the other colors in the painting, away from Annie herself. Just like the toy dog in the other painting, his little black beady eyes seemed to fasten onto mine. Maisie had painted them like the others: spinning vortexes, drawing me in. My stomach lurched and then I was falling into the deep, dark whirlpool of the dog's eyes, and I could hear him barking, far away, and the sound of squealing brakes.

I was on my knees on a rough wooden floor. It was dark. I could smell paint. I felt sick to my stomach, like I was going to throw up.

Slowly I got to my feet. I could see the dim outline of a window on the far wall. I groped around on a table and my hands closed on a box of matches. When I got one lit, I could see I was in Maisie's studio, and there was a candlestick sitting on the table.

The painting of Annie when she was five stood on the floor, leaning against the wall, with the other Annie paintings propped up beside it. I brought the candle over to look at it more closely.

I was right about the dog. It was the focus of the painting, not Annie, a darkness at the center. I looked at the next picture, which was Annie standing at a kitchen table, making cookies. She grinned out at me, with a couple of gobs of cookie dough on her face. Behind her, on a windowsill, stood a black china Scottie dog with spinning eyes. Once I started looking at him, his dark presence seemed to cast a shadow on the rest of the painting. I moved closer and then my foot caught on the first painting, and it fell over with a loud thud.

"Hello?" called a sleepy voice from the next room. Maisie.

I looked around for somewhere to hide, then remembered she couldn't see me. But could she touch me? I put the candle back on the table, blew it out, and then tucked myself into the corner near the window beside a tall dresser and stayed very still. I heard her fumbling with a key in the lock, and then the door opened.

"Claire?" she said. "Are you in here?"

I held my breath. Maisie stood there for a moment, then crossed to the table and lit the candle. She held it high, looking around the room.

"Claire!" she said sharply. Then she bent over and picked up the painting that had fallen over, setting it back in place against the wall. She stood there for a moment, looking down at it.

"Annie," she whispered, with a big sigh. She began to walk slowly around the room with the candle, peering into the corners. I tried to shrink back against the wall but there was nowhere for me to go.

She stopped in front of me. She looked right through me. I got that strange feeling again, like maybe I wasn't really there. Like maybe I really was a ghost.

Maisie shivered. The candle flickered, sending eerie shadows dancing over her face. She had a wide mouth and prominent cheekbones. She didn't look like Claire at all, except for her blueberry eyes, which seemed to be boring into mine.

"Annie," she whispered again, almost to herself.

And I felt suddenly that I knew this woman, inside and out. It was more than just her paintings—I knew her as well as I knew anybody.

"Maisie," I whispered, without thinking.

She heard me. I could see it in her face as she jumped back, and dropped the candle.

PART SEVEN

THE THEFT

"It's always tea-time."

The Mad Hatter,
ALICE'S ADVENTURES IN WONDERLAND

CLAIRE

DON'T KNOW WHAT woke me up. A voice, perhaps? I was suddenly wide awake, sitting up in my bed. It was mostly dark, except for a faint glow from the window that meant the sun would be up soon.

I heard Maisie's door open and footsteps go along the hall to her studio. I slipped out of bed and eased my door open to peek. I could just make out Maisie in her white nightgown, on her tiptoes, reaching up to the lintel above the door to her studio. She groped around for a moment, found what she was looking for, then I could hear a key jiggle against the lock as she opened the door.

"HA!" I thought to myself. "Gotcha!"

She put the key back up on the lintel and went into the room. I crept along behind her and then froze as she called my name. I held my breath. But she didn't come back into the hall, so I went up to the door and peered around the corner.

Maisie lit a candle and called my name again. She sounded cross. She started pacing through the room with the candle, looking for something. Then I saw Annie. She was pressed up against the wall beside the dresser, looking scared.

Maisie stopped in front of Annie. She whispered something I couldn't hear, and Annie had the strangest look on her face, like she couldn't believe what she was seeing. Then Annie whispered something back, and Maisie jumped back and dropped the candle. The room was plunged into darkness.

I could feel someone pushing past me into the hall.

"Maisie?" I called out.

"I'm here," she replied from inside the room. She fumbled around on the floor and then stumbled over to the table. I could hear her pushing things around, and then the sharp crack of a match striking as she relit the candle.

"What happened?" I asked.

"I don't know." Maisie was looking at me warily. "Were you asleep?"

"Yes. I heard you get up and came out to see what was going on."

"And you haven't been in here tonight?"

"No. What happened?"

Maisie looked away. "I thought I heard a noise in here. Maybe a mouse."

"Oh. Well, I'm going back to bed." I turned quickly so she wouldn't see the smile on my face. A mouse indeed. The haunting of Maisie was going very well.

There was a largish lump in my bed. I got in and wiggled my bare toes against Annie's, the way we used to. She laughed softly and wiggled hers back.

"What happened?" I whispered. "Maisie is really spooked!"

"Yes. A painting fell over, and she came in and started searching around the room. She stopped right by me—I think that cold spot thing was happening again."

"What were you whispering?"

"She said 'Annie' and I said 'Maisie.'"

"Did you say anything about the paintings?"

"I didn't have a chance. She dropped the candle."

"Next time you gotta tell her. Tell her you're back because of the paintings. You don't want them to be shown."

Annie didn't say anything.

"Annie?" I said, giving her a poke. "Did you hear me? You have to tell her not to show the paintings."

"I—I don't know," said Annie.

"What do you mean you don't know? That was the plan."

"I know, but that was before I saw her. It was just a game, getting her to believe she was haunted. But now that it's starting to work—"

"Now that it's starting to work is when you have to move in and deliver the goods, Annie! That was the whole point of haunting her."

"I know. But now it seems . . . it seems kind of mean."

"What?" I couldn't believe what I was hearing.

"It seems mean to play a trick on her. To make her think her dead daughter has come back to tell her not to show those paintings."

"But you have come back! And you don't want her to show the paintings, do you?"

Annie hesitated. "I don't know. They're so good."

I jumped out of bed. "Annie, don't do this to me. You said you would help."

"And I want to help, but I don't feel right about tricking Maisie. She's too sad."

"She's sad? What about what's going to happen to me when those paintings get shown? I'll be known all around the world as the girl who let her sister get killed!"

"It won't be like that, Claire. I promise. Get Maisie just to leave you out of it, like she said, and it doesn't have to come up."

"NO!" I wanted to scream but I knew it would wake Maisie up again. I leaned in close to Annie and spoke very carefully.

"I don't want those paintings shown. It's a betrayal of me and you and everything that happened. It's private. Maisie shouldn't be opening it up like that so everyone can see. Are you going to help me or not?"

"I want to help you, Claire, but isn't there another way? Besides the haunting?"

I closed my eyes and tried to think. My head was pounding again.

"There is one way," I said. "But you might not like it."

ANNIE

THE LIGHT FROM the window was slowly getting stronger. I could almost see Claire's face.

"If the paintings aren't here," she said, "Maisie can't show them."

"What do you mean, 'if they aren't here'? Where would they be?"

"Hidden. If we took them away, and hid them where no one could find them—"

"Maisie would know you'd taken them."

"So what is she going to do? Torture me?" Claire laughed.

I thought back to what I'd seen in Maisie's face a little while ago in the studio. Strength. Determination. I shivered. "Hopefully not," I said, and Claire laughed again.

"Look, I can hold out against her. She'll be mad. But there won't be anything she can do. Maybe she'll be so mad she'll want to get rid of me and let me go and live in St. John's. Two birds—one stone."

"I don't know," I said uncertainly. "She might just lock you in your room and throw away the key."

"I don't care," said Claire. "As long as she doesn't show those paintings."

"And where are you going to put them? It can't be damp. Or cold. It has to be safe."

"I've got the perfect hiding place," said Claire, her eyes

lighting up. "I found it a long time ago and Maisie would never guess. It's completely dry and warm."

"Where is it?"

"I'll show you. But we have to be very, very quiet."

She took a flashlight from her dresser and led me out into the dark hall, taking one careful step at a time, listening for any signs of life in Maisie's room. She opened the hall closet door and we slipped in, closing the door silently behind us. Claire turned on the flashlight and grinned at me.

"You're going to love this, Annie," she whispered.

We walked past the shelves of sheets and pillowcases and blankets, the hanging coats and the winter clothes, until we came to the far end and the door to the Mirror House. Claire slowly turned the handle and we were in.

There was a faint pink light coming in the window that faced east, over the ocean. The sun was coming up. Claire took me along the hall, passing the dark open doorways of the bedrooms. I shivered. I imagined the spirits of all the people who had lived in this house over the years, the lighthouse keepers, their wives and children, lingering, drifting, echoes of a time long past. I hurried to catch up with Claire, who was halfway down the stairs.

She waited for me at the bottom of the stairs, her face shining.

"This is so cool, Annie. I found it one day when I dropped a pen down the stairs. It landed on this step." She knelt down and pointed to the third step from the bottom. "I noticed this kind of crack at the back, see?"

There was a dark line just where the step met the riser. "Yes."

"I ran my finger along and this whole piece of wood started to jiggle." She pushed against the riser and it moved back. "You can see there's a space back there, right? But it won't move any more than that.

"It just so happened that I was reading a Philomena Faraday book that had a secret passage in an old house, and you opened it by turning a piece of carving beside an old fireplace. So I looked around, and lo and behold!" She took my hand and led me down the stairs. "There are these carved fish on the side of the staircase."

The fish looked like they were swimming up the stairs, one fish for every step.

"So I just started fooling around, trying to see if any of the fish would move, and—here, you try it."

I reached out to the third fish up and gave it a twist. Sure enough, it turned sideways with a satisfying click.

"Hey presto!" said Claire, dragging me round the bannister to look at the stairs.

The loose riser had flipped up, revealing a hidden shelf, built into the stairs, about seven inches tall and two and a half feet wide.

"Wow!" I said. "That is so cool." I bent over to peer in. "How far back does it go?"

Claire shone the flashlight in. The shelf went way back.

"Far enough to hide a painting in," she said.

CLAIRE

"**I**SN'T IT THE PERFECT hiding spot?" I said to Annie. "And every one of these stairs has one."

"What were they for?" asked Annie.

"There's a little cove along the shore just big enough to land a boat if the tides are right. It's called Smuggler's Cove. Ed told me that back in the 1920s, during Prohibition, fishermen used to smuggle in liquor from Saint-Pierre and Miquelon. Ed said that there are stories about how they used to have all kinds of hiding places in old root cellars and even here in the lighthouse. They'd hide the bottles until it was safe to take them away and sell. I figure someone built these shelves into the stairs so they could hide bottles here."

"And every stair has one?"

"Yup. I'll show you." I reached through the bannisters and twisted the fish on the fourth stair. The riser flipped up.

Annie took the flashlight and walked down the stairs and shone it along the side of the staircase. "So there's no other opening? They go right back to the wall?"

"Yup. They get shorter as they get closer to the top. But there's lots of room for the four Annie paintings."

"I guess," Annie said.

"They'll be safe. It's warm and dry. And Maisie will never find them."

Annie was silent.

"What's wrong?"

"I just don't feel right about it. Hiding her work."

"It won't be forever. Once she agrees not to have the show, I'll tell her where they are."

"I don't think it's going to be that easy to get Maisie to do something she doesn't want to."

"She's not taking me seriously. She's got to see how important this is for me."

"But I don't think you see how important it is for Maisie to show the paintings. She's not going to just give in to you."

"Whose side are you on, Annie?" I felt a sharp, throbbing pain above my right eye. "Do you want to help me or not?"

"Of course I want to help you. But I'm trying to show you what you're up against. I'm not sure that getting Maisie mad is the best way to go about getting what you want."

The pain was getting worse. I clutched my head and closed my eyes. I felt Annie's hands on my shoulders.

"Claire, what's wrong?"

"My head," I gasped. "I've got this bad headache; it keeps coming back."

She steered me over to the stairs and sat me down. Gently, she pulled my hands away from my head and placed her warm hands over my eyes.

"Take a deep breath," she said. "Keep breathing. In and out."

At first my breath was shaky, and I couldn't get a lungful of air. But after a couple of breaths, I started to relax a bit.

"In and out," said Annie softly. I could feel the warmth from her hands spreading into my head, surrounding the pain, loosening the knot. As we sat there, I began to feel the warmth going through my whole body, and then there was a pinky-red light all around me. I opened my eyes and Annie's hands fell away. The rising sun had bathed the hall in a warm glow.

Annie smiled at me. "Better?"

I rubbed my forehead. "Yes. Almost completely gone. How did you do that?"

"That's what I always do when you have a headache," said Annie. "Works every time."

"But—but you've never done that before," I said. "What do you mean?"

Annie's smile dropped and she stood up suddenly. "I meant, that's what I do when my mom in Toronto has a headache. It works for her, so I thought it would work for you." She walked down the hall toward the window where the sun was streaming in.

"It's so beautiful," she said. "It's making a path over the water. A shining path."

I stood up and started walking toward her. She was a dark shape, outlined by light. And then she disappeared.

ANNIE

I T WAS AS if the sky had unlocked and opened up to allow the sun to roll in, a red ball of fire that was laying down a golden path along the water. I had never seen anything so beautiful, and I felt like I was being welcomed home by a big warm mother who would stretch out her arms and enclose me in a gigantic hug. And then it all spun together in a fiery whirlwind that caught me up and twirled me around till I was dizzy and sick and everything went black.

"Annie?" said a gentle voice that I thought I recognized but couldn't quite place. A papery-soft hand touched my arm. I opened my eyes.

Mrs. Silver was sitting in the chair beside me, her hand on my arm, looking very concerned.

"Are you all right, dear?" she asked.

I looked around. We were all alone in the quiet corner of the library, with the leaves nodding slowly in the park outside and a few birds skittering past the window.

I felt awful. My head was still spinning and my stomach was lurching.

"You've been asleep for a long time," said Mrs. Silver.

I looked at my watch. It was five o'clock. I jumped up.

"I've got to get back. If I'm not home by four, Magda starts worrying." I swayed, and sat down again. "Whoa," I said, closing my eyes tight.

"What about a nice cup of tea?" said Mrs. Silver.

I opened my eyes again. Mrs. Silver was reaching into a green, quilted bag and pulling out a thermos.

"I find it usually does the trick," she said, unscrewing the top and pouring steaming brown tea into it. "Milk and sugar, isn't that how you like it?"

I nodded, taking the cup and sipping it slowly, my eyes never leaving her face. How did Mrs. Silver know how I took my tea? And why did she keep showing up wherever I went? She dived into her bag again and brought out a plastic ziplock bag full of cookies.

"Oatmeal and raisin," she said, offering me one. "Good for restoring your energy."

"What are you doing here?" I asked after a while, as the tea started to warm me up and the cookie made me feel a bit less like a wraith. "I was looking for you at the other library this morning. I didn't know you came here too."

"Oh yes, once in a while, when I have a particular interest," she said, her eyes twinkling at me. "It's one of my favorite places to go in the city. So convenient, right on the subway. And so many books!" She waved at the shelves of books all around us.

I laughed. I couldn't help it. She was so enthusiastic.

"So, down to business," she said. "How is your dear mother?"

"Not good. She wants to steal Maisie's paintings and hide them. I think she's heading for trouble because Maisie is unpredictable; she's a bit wild and—" I stopped, realizing what I was doing. "Oh. Did you mean my mother in hospital? Or my mother in—"

Mrs. Silver gave her head a little shake. "It's the same thing, Annie. She needs you. You need to keep going down there with her and help her find her way out."

"Down where?" I asked. "Down into Crooked Head?"

"Down into her dreams," replied Mrs. Silver.

I looked at the book, which had fallen to the floor. "I need the paintings in that book to get there," I said. "The ones in my other book don't work anymore."

"Then take it with you," said Mrs. Silver.

My mouth fell open. "You mean steal it?"

"Borrow it, shall we say?" said Mrs. Silver with a small smile. "This is a library, after all."

"But it's a reference book. You're not allowed to take them out. And there are security guards at the exits who check everyone's bags."

"Not mine," said Mrs. Silver, picking up the book. "I'm practically a fixture I'm here so often. And I volunteer for the reading program. They never check my bag."

The big book disappeared into her quilted bag. She took the thermos cup from me and screwed it back onto the thermos.

"Meet me across the street in five minutes," she said with a wink, and walked sedately down the aisle of books toward the elevators.

CLAIRE

IT WAS STILL too early to get up for school so I went back to bed. I lay there with the rosy light from the sun filling my room, thinking about when I could steal the paintings. It would have to be when Maisie was out. I'd have to make my preparations and then just be ready to grab my chance. She often was out when I got back from school, picking up things at the store or visiting some of her friends who lived along the shore. Or off sketching something. The problem was, I never knew how long she would be. She'd usually come back in time to make supper, so I might have a couple of hours. But she was unpredictable.

I'd stolen things from Maisie before. And she'd never found out. Every year when she painted the Annie picture, she made all kinds of sketches before she started painting. They were piled in drifts on her worktable. I went through and took two or three . . . not too many because I didn't want her to realize they were gone. Then I brought them back to my room to put in Annie's sketchbook.

The sketchbook was the one thing of Annie's that I kept. Maisie never knew I had it to begin with, and I've kept it hidden from her all these years. It's a hardcover book, as big as one of my school notebooks, but way thicker, filled with heavy white paper. Maisie gave it to Annie a week before she died. She made a big fuss about it being a "grown-up" sketchbook, and Annie was very excited about it.

Maisie was working a lot that summer, up in her studio, and Annie and I were left to our own devices. Sometimes we went to Nan's, but often we just hung out in our living room or the backyard. We would make cookies, play with dolls and do normal little kid things, but Annie also liked to spend time drawing. I liked reading, so we were often quiet together for an hour or so: Annie absorbed in her pictures and me in my books.

She didn't draw anything in her new sketchbook until the day before the accident. She told me she was waiting till she found something really special for the first picture. That day she opened it up and laid it on the coffee table and began to draw, with that weird focus she had that shut everything else out, her tongue sticking out slightly between her lips. I was reading *The Secret Garden* and I was lost on the Yorkshire moors and the creepy old house with sour-faced Mary. I liked Mary. She reminded me of—well, me.

I didn't pay much attention to Annie. She was quiet, so I could relax until she got it into her head to jump up and do something else.

After a while she called my name. I looked up, dragging myself away from the echoing halls of Misselthwaite Manor. Annie had a big smile on her face.

"Claire, want to see?" She held out the sketchbook to me.

I put my book down, stretched and went over to look.

I caught my breath. She had drawn a picture of me curled up in the overstuffed arm chair, bent over my book, completely absorbed, the curtain blowing in the window behind me.

Annie's drawing was always vivid and confident. Her technique was streets ahead of any other child her age—Maisie said she was a prodigy and I think she was right. Annie loved to show me her drawings and I was always taken aback at how sophisticated they were. Even with my lack of interest in art I knew she was something special.

But in this picture Annie had jumped ahead again. You could almost see the curtain moving with the wind, and she'd caught my likeness completely, down to the shape of my nose and the flowers on my T-shirt. And although I was very still in the drawing, you could tell I was lost in the book. The drawing had a feeling about it, a feeling of that warm summer day, a sense of peace.

Annie grinned at me and I gave her a big hug and told her she was a genius, and we both laughed, then we went to make lemonade.

The next day, after the accident, Mrs. Dearing, our neighbor, brought me into the living room while the ambulance screamed outside and the sunshine broke into sharp fragments of glass all around me. The first thing I saw was Annie's sketchbook, lying on the coffee table. I picked it up and hugged it to my chest. Later, when Nan came, I wouldn't let go of it and I took it to her house. I hid it under the bed.

Maisie never found out that Annie had drawn in her new sketchbook. I kept it secret. If she had seen it, she would have taken the sketch and put it in the big leather portfolio where she kept all Annie's work. I didn't want her to have it. Annie had done it for me.

When we went to Crooked Head, once I moved into my own room, I slept with the sketchbook clutched in my arms for months. I felt that a little part of Annie was preserved in that book. The book held the memory of the way Annie was that afternoon, completely caught up in her drawing, and then laughing with delight at her creation and my reaction as she bounced into the kitchen after me. I hugged that memory close and sometimes, just before I fell asleep, it was not the hard-edged book but Annie, soft and warm cuddling up to me. The next morning, I would hide the book away in an old suitcase under my bed with a bunch of dress-up clothes.

Over the years I pasted things into the book that reminded me of Annie. First there was her obituary from the newspaper and a short article about the accident that they printed with Annie's photograph. Then I slipped a few photographs of her out of our family albums and glued them in. Every year at Christmas I went through the Eaton's catalogue, the way Annie and I used to do, choosing what we would ask Santa for that year. I'd choose some toys and clothes I thought Annie would like, cut them out and paste them in the sketchbook. And every year I'd steal some of Maisie's working sketches of Annie. I always chose drawings of Annie's face.

I liked to sit with the book, turning from page to page. Feeling that Annie was with me.

That she wasn't gone forever.

ANNIE

Mrs. silver was right where she said she would be, across the street in front of the office supply store.

"Let's walk a bit, so it doesn't look too obvious," she said.

We walked down Yonge Street toward the subway. There were lots of people rushing by, and I had to keep alert not to bump into any of them. Mrs. Silver seemed to be a bit teeter-tottery, like she was going to lose her balance, so I got her to tuck her arm into mine and we walked along together. She looked happily around at everything, smiling, like it was all a wonderful show put on just for her. We stopped in front of the subway entrance.

"I won't come with you, dear. I want to go and look for some pretty handkerchiefs in The Bay. Do you know, handkerchiefs are so hard to find these days? And they're so much softer than Kleenex, and more ladylike, I think." She reached into her bag and pulled out the art book.

"There, now I just look like your grandmother giving you a

book, and not a desperate criminal passing on the goods," she said, with a tinkly little laugh.

"Thank you," I said. Then she turned and tottered away. She was soon swallowed up by the crowd.

When I got home, Magda was beside herself.

"Annie, oh, Annie, where have you been? Your father's been calling and I've been so worried about you." She gathered me in one of her vanilla-scented hugs. "With your poor mother taking a turn for the worse and—oops!" She clapped her hand over her mouth. "There I go with me big mouth flapping in the wind."

I felt the familiar clutch in my stomach. "Has something happened? Since last night?"

"Oh, well, it should be your father that tells you, but now I've let it out I better go on with it. Seems she had some kind of episode this afternoon, where she was having some pain and crying out. She stabilized after that but she's still on the ventilator . . . Oh dear, I shouldn't have told you," she wailed as I swayed and nearly fell down. She grabbed me and led me into the kitchen and pushed me into a chair.

"Head between your knees, Annie, let the blood come back." She pushed at the back of my neck until I bent my head over. I could feel the blood rushing back, pounding in my temples. I felt sick. I shook off her arm and sat up.

"Oh, goodness," she said. "You went as white as a sheet. I've heard people say that but I've never seen it. It's all my fault, bursting out with it like that. Here, have a glass of water."

I sipped at the water.

"But is she okay?"

"She's fine now. Your father says it might mean that she's struggling to wake up. And that's a good thing."

At Magda's suggestion, I went up to my room for a "wee nap." She told me my father would be home for dinner at 7:30.

That gave me about an hour to get back to Crooked Head.

I shut my door and sat on the bed. Then I opened the book.

The painting after *Annie I* was the painting of Annie standing in front of the lighthouse dressed in a sweater with a black Scottie dog knitted into it. Again, the image of the Scottie was disturbing and took away from Annie's bright smile and the sunny day. A dark beacon in the midst of a happy day. I wondered if a person who didn't know about Annie's accident would find the picture as unsettling as I did. The dog was so weird looking, with those strange eyes—I looked closer. Yes, they were painted as spinning vortexes again. My dizziness came rushing back and then I was falling.

This time I was turning head over heels and then I landed with a thump.

"Annie!" cried Claire. "You're just in time!"

CLAIRE

I HAD JUST LAID out an old blanket on the floor and placed one of the Annie paintings on it, the one where she's standing at the kitchen table mixing cookie dough, when Annie fell into the studio beside me.

"Annie! You're just in time! Maisie's out somewhere but I don't know how long she'll be. We need to be quick."

Annie struggled to her feet. She looked around the room, then walked over to the painting of Annie standing in front of the lighthouse. She bent down to look at something.

"Annie!" I said. "I need help with this."

She turned back to me and focused on what I was doing with the painting.

"Not a blanket," she said. "A sheet would be better."

"Oh rats! I collected all these old blankets from the Mirror House."

"Go find some sheets," said Annie. "They're cleaner and better for the paintings."

I ran out of the studio into the hall closet and pulled some old sheets from a shelf.

"Here," I said, thrusting them into Annie's arms. She was standing looking down at the painting with a dazed expression on her face.

We spread out a sheet and got the painting wrapped up.

"Let's hide this one first," I said. "So if she comes home early, at least one will be hidden."

Annie agreed and we carried it together along the hall, through the closet and down the stairs. I turned the fish on the fourth step and we slid the painting in. Then I turned the fish and the riser fell back into place.

"She'll never find it," I said. "Let's go get another."

A door slammed next door, and I could hear Maisie calling out, "Claire, are you home?"

I grabbed Annie's arm. "Oh no, she's back! What should we do?"

Annie took charge, just the way she did when I set the kitchen on fire. "You go and talk to her, keep her downstairs. I'll clear up the studio and put the key back."

"Can you get another painting? Or take all of them? It's not going to work if we only have one."

"I'll try," said Annie, and then we both sped up the stairs, into the closet and along to the door at the end. I burst through and nearly knocked Maisie down the stairs.

"Watch it, Claire," she said, grabbing the bannister. "What's the hurry? And what were you doing in the closet? Were you in the Mirror House?"

Annie slipped by, heading for the studio.

"I was just . . . just . . . looking around."

"You know you're not supposed to go over there."

Behind Maisie, the studio door closed silently.

"I've taken all the Annie paintings into my studio, if that's what you were looking for," said Maisie.

There was a tremendous crash from the studio. Maisie whirled around and strode over to the door. She glanced at me, and tried the handle. It opened.

I followed her in. The Annie paintings had all fallen over. The window was wide open. Annie stood in the corner, trying to shrink into the wall.

"What on earth?" said Maisie. "I left this door locked. And the window shut. What have you been up to, Claire?"

She began setting the paintings upright, and then noticed the blankets and the sheets. "Claire? What were you doing?"

I didn't say anything. She turned and looked at the paintings.

"Where's the one with the cookies?"

I just looked at her.

"Claire? Where is it?"

"I took it. I don't want you showing those paintings. I told you. You wouldn't listen."

"And you think you're going to stop me by hiding the paintings? And playing tricks on me, pretending to be Annie's ghost?"

"I didn't—" I began.

"Don't lie to me, Claire!" said Maisie. "I'm sick and tired of all your nonsense. I'm showing these paintings, no matter what, and you're not going to stop me by stealing them or by leaving books about ghosts beside my bed. Now tell me where the painting is."

I looked at her for a moment. Then I said, "No."

She took a step toward me, "Claire, this has gone far enough. Where is the painting?"

I turned and walked toward the door.

She was after me in a second, grabbing me by the back of my shirt. She spun me around and gave me a shake.

"Tell me where it is or I'll—"

"You'll what?" I said. "Hit me? Beat it out of me? Go on. I dare you!"

She glared at me, for a moment, then she let go. She took a couple of deep breaths, as if she was trying to calm herself down.

"Claire, I've told you. I won't mention you in any of the reference material. I'll keep you out of it. I won't say anything about the accident. You won't come into it. But I need to show these paintings. This is my work, Claire."

"That's all you care about, isn't it? Your work. You don't care about me or how I feel and you never cared about Annie either. It was your fault that she died, not mine! You shouldn't have left us on our own that day, but you had to do your precious work. You blame me, but we both know that it was your fault."

She slapped me then, hard across my face. Then her face crumpled and she covered her mouth with her hand.

I put my hand to my face where she hit me. There was a kind of ringing in my head.

"Claire," she said, reaching out her arms to me. "I'm sorry, I'm sorry."

I took a step back. "Stay away from me. I hate you!" And then I turned and fled to my room.

ANNIE

THE SOUND OF the slap seemed to echo through the room after Claire left. Maisie dropped to her knees and covered her face with her hands.

"Annie," she sobbed. "Annie," and then she held her stomach as if she had a bad pain.

I couldn't bear it. I went over to her and knelt down and put my arms around her.

"It's okay, Maisie," I whispered. "I'm here."

She kept crying, rocking back and forth, and I kept hugging her, for a long time. I was dimly aware of a breeze coming in the window, seagulls crying outside, and the waves crashing against the rocks below the lighthouse, but Maisie and I were in our own world. I wasn't sure if she could feel my touch, but I think that in some deep part of her she could sense my presence.

Finally she stopped crying and I moved away. She dried her eyes and turned to look at the paintings of Annie behind her.

After a few moments she got wearily to her feet and headed out of the studio and down the hall, with me trailing along behind. She knocked at Claire's door, and then went in.

Claire was sitting in the big chair, staring out the window.

"Claire," said Maisie. "I shouldn't have hit you. I'm sorry."

Claire turned to look at her. One side of her face was still burning red.

"We need to talk. About Annie. About what happened that day. We've left it too long."

"No!" said Claire, jumping to her feet. "There's nothing to talk about. We both know what happened."

"It was an accident," said Maisie. "It wasn't my fault. It wasn't your fault. It just happened."

"That's not true," said Claire, her lower lip trembling. "You think it was my fault. I know you do. You blame me. You think I should have stopped her from running."

Maisie shook her head. "No. I don't. I know how she ran."

"You're lying. I see it every time you look at me. You blame me and you wish it was me that died, not Annie!"

"No," said Maisie, moving toward her, her voice breaking. "No, Claire. No."

"Let me out of here," begged Claire. "Let me go to Nan's. You don't want me."

"Claire, that's not true. I love you. I love you just as much as I loved Annie."

"Then prove it," said Claire. "Don't show the paintings. I'm asking you. For my sake."

Maisie shook her head. "I won't be blackmailed by you, Claire. The paintings are my art. They are my work. I can't stop the clock. They have to be shown."

"Well you won't be showing the one with the cookies. It's gone forever."

"What do you mean? What have you done with it?"

"You'll never see it again," said Claire, standing up and facing her mother. "I burned it. In the stove. I burned it while you were away."

I gasped. Why was she saying that?

Maisie took a step back, as if Claire had struck her.

"You burned my painting? How could you do that, Claire?"

"To show you once and for all that it's a painting! It's not a human being. I'm standing right in front of you and you don't care about me. You care more about your paintings than you do about me. You don't love me. You didn't love Annie. All you care about is your paintings. I'd burn all of them if I could."

Maisie stood perfectly still. Then she took a deep breath and spoke in a tight, controlled voice.

"You don't know what you've done," she said. "You'll regret this one day, Claire. And it's not going to stop my show. I'll show the ones I have. And meanwhile you can go and live with Nan. It will be better for both of us right now to be apart. I'll call Nan now and see if she will come out and pick you up." Then she turned and left the room.

Claire stood looking after her mother. Then she began to cry. I moved toward her but my legs were suddenly heavy and the room darkened, as if a cloud had covered the sun. She looked up at me and reached out her arms but even though I was trying with all my strength to move toward her, she was getting farther and farther away from me instead of closer. Then she blinked into darkness and I could still hear her crying, but I was falling again, falling out of the lighthouse, bouncing down over the rocks, falling deep into the ocean, swallowed up by waves of darkness.

CLAIRE

'D DONE IT. I'd got what I wanted. Maisie was letting me go. I would move to St. John's and live with Nan.

So why did I feel like my heart was broken in two? I saw Annie standing at the door, looking scared and white. I called out to her and she started toward me, and then it was like a dark cloud descended into the room, and then she stretched out her arms to me, but she was getting farther and farther away from me, then she blinked into nothing and I was alone.

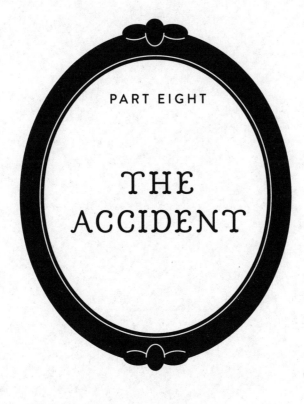

PART EIGHT

THE ACCIDENT

"Only it is so very lonely here!" Alice said in a melancholy voice; and at the thought of her loneliness two large tears came rolling down her cheeks.

THROUGH THE LOOKING-GLASS,
AND WHAT ALICE FOUND THERE

ANNIE

WHEN I CAME to, a bell was ringing. I opened my eyes. I was lying on my bed, the book open beside me to the painting of Little Annie standing outside the lighthouse. I sat up. I felt terrible. My mouth was dry and I was so dizzy I had to close my eyes for a minute. The bell stopped ringing and I could hear Magda talking downstairs. Talking on the phone. The bell must have been the phone.

I opened my eyes again. Why was it getting harder every time? It was scary, falling like that. And I felt so heavy and dragged out. Like I had the flu.

There were footsteps coming up the stairs. I shut the book. Magda knocked on the door.

"Come in," I said.

She stepped into the room and I knew right away something was wrong. It was written all over her face.

"I'm sorry, love," she said. "That was your dad on the phone. Your mom isn't doing very well. He wants me to bring you to the hospital."

CLAIRE

M Y HEAD WAS pounding. I wanted nothing more than to crawl into bed and close my eyes. But instead I pulled out the old suitcase from under my bed. I took out Annie's sketchbook and laid it carefully on my pillow. Then I started to pack.

I took piles of underwear, shirts and socks out of my drawers and put them neatly into the suitcase. Sweaters, jeans, shorts. My bathing suit. There was a pool near Nan's. Maybe it would be warm enough to go swimming in a few weeks. I stood by my bookcase and frowned. What books to bring? I couldn't bring all of them. Just a couple of favorites. There was a library not too far away from Nan's place. I could go every day if I wanted to.

A sob shook through me. I was starting to cry again. I felt raw, like I'd drunk some horrible poison that burned my insides. I wiped away my tears and reached for *Emily of New Moon* and *Anne of Green Gables*. I was just about an orphan now, so I might as well read books about orphans. I sniffed.

Suddenly there was a knock on my door and Maisie came in.

"I've just talked to Nan," she said, crossing over to my bed. "She can be here tomorrow. She's not very happy about the situation—" Maisie broke off. "What's this?" she said, reaching for the sketchbook.

I cried out and tried to grab it from her but she whisked it away and took it to the window, where the light poured in. She opened it. Then she made a kind of strangled noise.

"Annie?" she said, looking over at me. "This is Annie's." She looked back at the book. I could see she was staring at the sketch Annie had made of me, the day before she died. Sitting in the armchair reading *The Secret Garden*.

"I've never seen this," she whispered, and turned the page.

"No!" I cried, going over and trying to get the book from her. "Don't look at it! It's mine!"

She held the book out of reach and glared at me. "You kept this from me? All this time? Annie's sketches?"

"No," I said, reaching for the book again. "There's only one. She only did one."

"But there's more in here," said Maisie, turning the pages. She flipped through the pages where I had glued newspaper clippings and the funeral program, and the cutouts from the Eaton's catalogue, till she got to the thicker pages where I'd glued in her sketches for the Annie paintings.

She stared at the first one. "This isn't Annie's," she said. "This is mine." She turned some more pages, then looked up at me, outraged. "You took these from my studio? You stole my work? So the painting of Annie wasn't the first? What else have you taken from me?"

"Nothing," I said. "Nothing."

But it wasn't true. I'd taken Annie from her.

ANNIE

D AD MET MAGDA and me at the elevators. I was so scared I could barely breathe. I was trying very hard to focus on one thing at a time and try not to think about Mom. Right now it was Dad's five-o'clock shadow, all those tiny little black bristles all over his cheeks and chin.

"Come in here, Annie," said Dad, taking my arm and leading me into the quiet room. Magda faded into the background. He sat me down in a chair and took my hand.

"What's happened," I whispered. "Is Mom dead?"

"No, no," he said quickly. "She's in a bit of trouble, but she's holding her own."

I was examining his tie, which had thin green stripes. The knot was crooked. Dad never messed up his tie. He was very particular about the way he looked.

"Then why did you ask Magda to bring me here?" I was still whispering.

"Your mother has been calling for you," he said.

I looked up then. His eyes were bloodshot from lack of sleep.

"She started to wake up, and she's breathing on her own without the ventilator. But she isn't fully conscious and her heartbeat is erratic. They've stabilized her but she isn't doing well, Annie. They did another MRI and found some bleeding in her brain. They need to operate."

I clutched his hand. "Dad—" I was so scared I couldn't say any more. My throat felt like it had closed up.

He put his other arm around me and drew me into a tight hug.

"Annie," he said into my hair. "Annie." His voice broke a little.

I could feel his heart beating steadily through his shirt. I clung to him. If his heart kept on beating like that, if Mom's heart kept on beating too, and mine, if we all just kept going it would be okay. I felt the circle again, the way I'd felt it that time when I laid my head down on her chest. Only this time Dad was in it too.

"It's actually good news, in a way," he said, pulling away a little and looking down at me. "She's waking up. And now they can see where the problem is. They can relieve the pressure and then she should . . . she should be okay. I've done dozens of these operations myself, Annie. She'll be okay."

I know he was trying to sound reassuring but he wasn't totally successful. I could feel him trembling.

"Can I see her?" I asked.

"Yes," he said, standing up. "There's just time before they prep her for the operation. I think it will do her good. She's been calling your name."

Mom looked paler than ever. The tube was gone from her mouth. The bank of small screens behind her hummed, casting a ghostly green light on her face.

"You've just got a few minutes," said Dad. "I'll leave you with her. I need to talk to Dr. Minto before the operation." He left.

I picked up her hand. It was cool.

"Mom," I said. "It's Annie. I'm here."

She didn't move. I leaned in closer. "Claire," I said. "It's Annie. I'm here."

Her eyelids flickered. Ever so slightly.

"Claire," I said. "I'm coming back as soon as I can. Hang on."

She opened her eyes and looked into mine. But she didn't look like Mom. She was Claire, twelve years old and frightened. She gripped my hand.

"Annie," she whispered. "I have to tell you about the accident. It was my fault. When you got hit. Maisie never found out." Then she gave a low moan and closed her eyes.

"Claire?" I said, "Claire?"

"Did she speak?" came my father's voice from over my shoulder. He pushed past me and picked up her wrist, taking her pulse, his eyes scanning the screens above the bed. Dr. Minto came in behind him.

"Yes," I said.

"Her heartbeat is erratic," he said to Dr. Minto.

"We need to go in right now," she replied.

230

I shrank back against the wall as a couple of nurses came hurrying in and they started doing things to Mom. I stumbled out of the room. Magda was standing outside the door, wringing her hands.

"Come," she said to me. "Let's get you home. We need to let the doctors look after your mom now."

Dad came out and had a quick word with Magda and then they were wheeling Mom down the hall on a stretcher. Dad leaned over and took me by the shoulders.

"She'll be okay, Annie," he said. "Go home with Magda. I'll call you as soon as there's any news."

I let Magda lead me to the elevators and then down the long white hall to the exit. She hailed a taxi and we sped home. Cars, traffic lights and houses streamed by, but I was blind to them. All I could see was Claire looking out of my mother's face.

CLAIRE

MAISIE GLARED at me.

"I'm taking this," she said, holding Annie's sketchbook. "And I'm going to go through it and I'm going to discover exactly what you've been keeping secret from me all these years."

"No!" I cried out. "You can't! It's private."

"I thought my work was private until I found out that you'd been spying on me and taking things out of my studio!"

"No, Maisie, this is different. You can't. You can't read it. No!"
I grabbed at the book and we struggled over it for a minute then
I gave her a big push, and while she was off balance, I wrenched
the book away from her and took off.

I tore down the stairs and burst out of the front door and ran.
Ran as fast as I could, as fast as Annie, over the rocks and the
tufts of grass and down the path, running. I could hear her calling me, but I kept running.

I got to the edge of the cliff, where I'd seen Annie in her red
shorts a couple of days before.

I looked back toward the lighthouse. It rose up, a red tower
against the bright-blue sky. My head throbbed. The pain was
almost unbearable now.

Maisie came crashing out of the woods.

I took the sketchbook and threw it as far as I could, out over
the ocean.

"NO! Claire, NO!" screamed Maisie. We watched as the
book bounced off some rocks at the bottom of the cliff and into
the water.

I turned to my mother. Her face was crumpling into tears.

"Claire—" she said. "Claire—Why would you do that? Annie's
last drawing?"

"I didn't want you reading it," I said. "It was mine."

We stood on the edge of the cliff, staring at each other. I felt
the world spinning, like we were locked in a moment in time that
would never end.

ANNIE

WHEN WE GOT home I went straight up to my room, once I convinced Magda that I couldn't eat supper and needed to be alone. I sat on my bed and looked at the painting of Newfoundland on my wall.

It was just as beautiful as ever. The road was so inviting—as if Maisie was saying come in, come here, come into this world and walk along the road to the lighthouse, and you will find something you have always wanted. I realized that that was what it always said to me. It was the promise of a different world, a world of heartbreaking beauty where everything was right and seabirds flew against the sky and the wind blew patterns in the tall grass.

But it wasn't really that wonderful world. Now I knew how unhappy Claire had been there.

No wonder she hid it away in the attic. She didn't want to be reminded of those sad years after Annie died, and her break with her mother. But I had hauled the painting down out of the attic and forced her to look at it again. Forced her to remember. I'd found her in my room a few times, sitting on the bed, staring at the painting with a lost look on her face.

Now that I thought about it, Mom had never been quite the same since I brought that painting down and put it up on my wall. She'd been more distant, more forgetful. The past was eating away at her.

CLAIRE

EVEN AS THE book hit the water I felt its loss. I could never look at Annie's sketch again and get back to that afternoon before she died, before everything went so dark. I could never look at those sketches I stole from Maisie, those sketches of Annie's sweet face. I could never turn the pages and look at the catalogue cutouts and read all the little fantasies I wrote about what it would be like if Annie had never died.

But I had to let it go. Maisie could never read it. Because I had written down exactly what happened the day Annie left us, and I never wanted Maisie to know the truth.

ANNIE

I OPENED THE BOOK of Maisie's paintings to the index at the back. Of course it was there. Right under *A. The Accident.*

The painting was framed by a window, with white curtains billowing at each side. It was the second floor of a house, over-looking a bright, sunny street with a row of jellybean-colored houses opposite. A big black car with a shiny silver grille across the front was stopped on an angle in the street below, and there was a bright-red pool of blood on the road in front of it. A little girl with light-brown hair and blue shorts stood on the curb, looking toward the pool of blood. Across the street

was the black Scottie dog with his whirling eyes. The blood was running down the road into a huge deep crack, where the road was split, as if there had been an earthquake. On this side everything was bright and shiny, and on the other the houses were gray.

I closed my eyes. I didn't want to go into that painting.

"Annie!"

Someone was calling me. I opened my eyes.

"Annie, come!" It was Claire, calling me the way she did that first night when I fell into the lighthouse painting. I had to go.

I looked at the painting. The Scottie dog started to bark. I fell.

CLAIRE

I HAD A FIGHT with Annie that day. And a fight with Maisie. I wanted to stay home and keep reading *The Secret Garden*. I was just at the part where Mary had found Colin crying in the middle of the night. I wanted to find out who he was. Maisie had promised to take us swimming that afternoon, but she kept putting it off. She was working on some painting and didn't want to stop.

Annie was bugging me, jumping up and down, talking about going swimming. She wouldn't leave me alone and let me read.

I yelled at her and then Maisie came down and yelled at me and told me to take Annie to get Popsicles and we'd go swimming later. I didn't want to go, but Maisie said I had to and that she couldn't work with Annie making so much noise and, "Just do what I ask, Claire, and don't always argue with me." Then she went stomping back upstairs to her studio.

So I put my book down and told Annie to come on and crashed out the door and down the steps and started walking really fast and Annie was calling out behind me to wait up.

ANNIE

I WAS STANDING AT an open window with white curtains billowing out in a summer breeze. Maisie was standing beside me, a paintbrush in her hand, looking down into the street.

A girl in blue shorts and a white T-shirt went running down the front steps and started walking quickly down the street. Claire.

"Claire, wait for me!" called a little girl, and Annie came jumping down the steps, brown curls flying.

Claire kept on going. Annie caught up with her and grabbed her arm and gave it a little shake.

"You're supposed to hold my hand, Claire. Maisie says. ALWAYS hold my hand."

Claire shook her off and kept walking.

"Leave me alone, you little brat," she said over her shoulder.

"You're not supposed to call me that," sang out Annie. "I'll tell Maisie."

A dog barked. A black Scottie appeared on the other side of the street. I opened my mouth to warn them but no sound came out.

"Sammy!" yelled Annie, and ran.

Right into the path of a big black car.

Claire lunged after her, yelling, "Annie, stop!"

The brakes squealed, and there was an awful thump. Then it seemed like everything just stopped.

I looked at Maisie. Her hands were over her mouth, and her eyes were full of so much terror and pain that I had to look away. Below us on the sidewalk Claire stood frozen, as if she'd been turned to stone.

The dog kept barking.

CLAIRE

I COULD NEVER TELL anyone what really happened. Never. Not Nan. Not Maisie. Not the police, or the psychiatrist. Nobody. I had killed my sister, as sure as if I'd pushed her in front of that car. If I had been holding her hand, she wouldn't have gotten away from me. She would still be alive.

I had to keep it a secret. From everyone except Annie. Those first few days when she came back to haunt me, I thought I would break down and tell Nan. Annie looked so sad. Every time I saw her it was like she was reproaching me. But once I yelled at her to leave she went away. And then I prayed that she would forgive me and come back.

And she did. That night when she came into my room, when I was cold and the moon was making a silver path across the sea. She wasn't mad. She was different: quiet and sad. But she had forgiven me. I know that's why she came back. To let me know she still loved me and to help me get away from Maisie.

ANNIE

I CLOSED MY EYES. And then the noise started. Outside someone was screaming and beside me Maisie started to make a horrible, strangled noise. I covered my ears with my hands. Then I felt dizzy and the familiar falling feeling started, and I felt like I would never hit the bottom of the endless darkness.

———

"Annie! Annie, can you hear me?"

I opened my eyes. Magda was leaning over my bed, looking very worried.

"Oh, thank goodness," she said. "You must have been having a terrible nightmare. Screaming your head off. You scared me clean out of my wits."

I sat up. My room was dark. The light from the hall cut a bright oblong across the floor. Magda sat down beside me and put her arms around me.

I clung to her. I couldn't get the image of that street in St. John's out of my head. The car.

The dog. Claire. Annie jumping down the steps. Claire.

When Claire first told me about the accident, she said she was holding Annie's hand, and that Annie had got away from her. But she wasn't holding her hand. And Maisie saw it happen. Claire kept it secret all these years, but Maisie knew all along. And she never said anything.

I pulled away from Magda.

"Is there any news about Mom?" I asked. Her eyes skittered away from mine.

"Your dad phoned. The operation went well but she . . . well, she had a little trouble with her heart."

"Is she—? Is she—?"

"She's okay; they got her stabilized. All they can do now is wait. Your dad is with her but he didn't want to wake you up."

"Oh." I lay back on the bed. The world was still spinning around me.

"Could you eat something now?" asked Magda.

I shook my head. "No." She was kind, and she was doing her best to make me feel better—but I needed to be alone. "I'll be okay. I'll probably go back to sleep."

Magda took a little more persuading, but she finally left.

I reached for the book and turned the page. I never wanted to look at the painting of the accident again. The next page showed the painting of Claire's room, the one with the red blanket hanging over the chair. The one called *Empty*, dated 1978. I wondered if Maisie painted it just after Claire went away to live with her Nan.

I turned the page.

It was a painting of Claire. She was my age, sitting on her bed, on my quilt, with a plate of oatmeal cookies beside her, a mug of what looked like hot chocolate on the bedside table. She was reading a book. I could even see the title, *The Eternal Shadow* by Philomena Faraday.

I'd seen the same book on her table the day we met on the causeway in the fog. The day we ate the oatmeal cookies on her bed.

Maisie had caught my mother's expression perfectly. I'd seen that tiny frown on her face so many times when she was deep in a book. A wisp of her hair fell over her cheek. I half expected her to reach out her hand and take a cookie.

But nothing moved in the painting. It was just Maisie's skill that made her seem so alive. The painting was called *Reading* and there was no mention of Claire in the caption.

I turned the page. There was Claire again, about nine years old, walking down the road with the lighthouse in the background. It was a lot like my lighthouse painting, but Claire was in the foreground, looking angry and sad, her face pinched. The painting was called *Banishment*, and again, there was no mention of Claire in the caption.

On the next page was a painting of Claire in front of a little trailer that had the word *Bookmobile* painted across the top. Her arms were full of books and she had a tiny smile on her face. It was called *Anticipation*. No mention of Claire.

Maisie had really seen her. She had painted her dissatisfaction, her loneliness, the way she could be totally absorbed in a book, the way she stood back from the world. Claire thought Maisie didn't love her and couldn't see her. But Maisie did. She couldn't help painting her, but she'd kept her name out of it. She'd given Claire her privacy.

Suddenly I understood everything. I knew why I had been going into the paintings, why I was inside my mother's dreams. I knew what I had to do.

PART NINE

THE CALL

"Well, now that we have seen each other,"
said the Unicorn, "if you'll believe in me,
I'll believe in you. Is that a bargain?"

THROUGH THE LOOKING-GLASS,
AND WHAT ALICE FOUND THERE

CLAIRE

THE MORNING AFTER I threw Annie's sketchbook away, Nan came and drove me to St. John's. I turned my back on Crooked Head and Maisie and made a new life with Nan. It was hard to keep Maisie shut out of my life, but I did my best. The first few times she came to visit I refused to speak to her. She went ahead with the show in New York of the Annie paintings. I never told her about the one I had hidden under the stairs.

After a while I started talking to Maisie again. It took too much energy to be silent around her. But I said as little as possible and kept my business to myself. Nan kept her updated about what I was doing. St. Brigid's was good for me. I reconnected with some of my old friends and made some new ones. I didn't do a lot of socializing—mostly I just worked. I had my eye on an English scholarship to the University of Toronto and I never wavered. I wanted to get as far away from Crooked Head and Newfoundland as I could and never go back.

Nan died my first year away at university. It was a heart attack: very sudden. I went home for the funeral. Maisie hugged me, weeping, but I didn't hug her back. I felt frozen inside.

Nan hated it that Maisie and I never made up. She split her money between us, and made Maisie the executor of her will. She set it up so I would get some money every year and Maisie had to be the one to send it to me. Nan knew that I would never be in touch with Maisie otherwise. I had to keep Maisie informed about what was happening to me with a letter every year before I could get the money.

I could have let it go. I mean, I needed the money in university, but after that, when I got my teaching job, I could have done without it. But by that time I had Annie, and I thought she should have Nan's inheritance, for her future. And maybe I didn't want to let go of that last thread that connected me to Maisie.

So every year I wrote a letter and told Maisie what was happening. She knew when I got my Ph.D., knew when I got married, knew when I had Annie. She sent me the painting of the lighthouse for a wedding present. And when Annie was born, she started sending presents for her birthday and Christmas, every year.

I couldn't give them to her. I hadn't even told Ron that my mother was alive. I had to keep Maisie secret. She sent the presents to a private post office box I kept for our correspondence, and I smuggled them home and hid them away in my old trunk from Crooked Head. I could have just thrown them away. But I didn't.

I opened each one as it came, careful not to rip the paper,

sitting on the floor in the attic. Maisie's drawings were so funny, and the things she had knit were so adorable. But I couldn't let her in. When I saw her handwriting and her drawings and those sweaters and hats and socks, I let all those old painful feelings rise up and then I pushed them all down again as I wrapped the present back up and put it in the trunk with the others. Someday maybe I would give them to Annie. Someday maybe I would tell her the whole story. But not yet.

When Annie found the painting, everything started to crumble. I couldn't take it away from her. And it seemed to have a strange power over me. I'd never looked at any of Maisie's paintings since I left Crooked Head, and now I couldn't pass Annie's room without looking at it. Then I found myself sitting on her bed, staring at it, with everything flooding back. The lighthouse. The ocean. The accident. The ghosts.

ANNIE

I OPENED MY DOOR and listened. I could hear the TV downstairs. I crept along the hall to Dad's study, went in and quietly closed the door. I crossed the room to his desk and picked up the phone.

It was easy. Dialing 411 got me information and they gave me a phone number for M. King in Crooked Head, Newfoundland. I dialed it.

It rang seven times. Then someone picked it up and a husky voice said, "Hello?"

It was Maisie. All of a sudden I froze. I didn't know what to say.

"Hello?" she repeated.

"Uh . . . hi. Umm . . . you don't know me. This is Annie. Annie Jarvis."

Silence.

Then, "Annie? Is that really you?"

"Yes! Yes, it's me. I know all about you, but my mother doesn't know I'm calling. Or my father."

"I—I don't understand. I'm so happy to hear from you but—"

"It's Claire," I blurted out. "She's really sick. Maisie, you have to come."

"Sick? What's wrong with her?"

"She . . . she had a car accident. She was in a coma and now she's had brain surgery and . . . and . . ." I stuttered to a stop. I felt the tears coming but I needed to tell her. "Maisie, she needs you. She's been worrying, all this time, about Little Annie. About the accident. Because she wasn't holding her hand and she never told you and she blames herself and please, please come. I don't want her to die. I think if she knew you were there and don't blame her for the accident . . . I think she might get better."

Silence.

"Annie . . . I . . . I don't know what to say. Did she tell you all this?"

"I can't explain. I just know. And I know that you love her. She loves you too, and she needs you. She always needed you. I think if you could just be there with her and talk to her, she would know that she doesn't have to keep punishing herself."

"It was an accident," said Maisie in a broken voice. "I know."

CLAIRE

ALL MY LIFE I felt like something inside me was broken. Long before the accident. Maisie was like a ball of fire rolling through my life, big, overpowering, hard to resist. I felt insignificant beside her. Unimportant. I couldn't be the daughter she wanted. I couldn't be Annie.

Annie never was daunted by Maisie the way I was. She had her own fiery energy, and she and Maisie burned happily together. I was always the odd one out, standing on the sidelines. And then when Annie died, it felt like a dark shadow fell over the world that only I could see. It went with me everywhere, and my mouth tasted of ashes.

Over the years the shadow receded. I built a new life in Toronto and closed the door on everything that connected me to

Newfoundland. I locked all the broken bits of myself away like the presents in that old trunk in the attic, and I thought they would never come to light.

Ron and I were happy together. I loved my job. When Annie was born, a light came into my life, and I thought it would keep the shadow away. I called her Annie because I thought she could take my sister's place. I thought she would heal me.

But it didn't happen like that. It was uncanny how much my Annie looked like Little Annie, but she wasn't like her at all. Except for drawing. All Annie wanted to do was draw, and she was very good, the way Little Annie was. But my Annie was strange and quiet and hard to reach. Ron insisted there was something wrong with her and kept hauling her into the hospital for tests. None of them came to anything. She just lived in her own quiet world where she needed to draw all the time. I think I knew for a long time that something was broken in her the way it was with me. She didn't fit with Ron and me. It was like she spoke a different language.

When Annie found the painting in the attic and hung it in her bedroom, I couldn't stop thinking about the past. I found myself dreaming about my childhood, and my sister, Annie, and Maisie. It was as if that room where I locked everything away had a big crack in the wall, and things were starting to spill out.

The day I had the accident was a difficult one for me. Every June 10 since Annie died has been difficult. But this one was worse than ever, because so many things had started to come to the surface in the last few months. I could see Annie in my mind, the way I did when I was at Crooked Head and longed for her ghost. She was always laughing, and running, full of enthusiasm. I could never catch up with her.

When I got in the car to drive home after my class, I was so tired I didn't think I could make it home. A heaviness descended upon me. I pulled myself together and began to drive. The streetlights picked out a winding path through the Don Valley. I followed them, trying not to think, and then they began to flicker.

One by one the lights went out, leaving the road in darkness. My car lights didn't seem to be working. I was driving blind through a deep darkness as thick as the blackest Newfoundland night. It felt like I had driven into one of my nightmares. I felt the tires leaving the road and the car was jerking and bouncing over rough ground. There was a tremendous crash and broken glass rained down on my head.

ANNIE

I DON'T KNOW HOW I got to sleep that night. Maisie said she would get a flight as soon as she could, but she didn't think she could be in Toronto before the evening of the next day. All I could think of was Mom, lying pale and still in the hospital bed. I tossed and turned.

I don't remember sleeping, but somehow it was morning and light was pouring into my room. I went downstairs to find Magda asleep on the couch, wrapped in a blanket. She woke up when she heard me and we had a very quiet breakfast together. The whole world seemed to be hushed, waiting.

Time ticked slowly by. I couldn't settle to anything, just wandered around the house. I kept coming back to my room and sitting on my bed, staring at the painting of the lighthouse. The painting that had started all of this. It still looked so alive. The colors jumped out at me, and I could almost smell the salt in the air, almost feel the breeze that ruffled the grasses. I closed my eyes and tried to focus all my energy on Mom.

"Claire," I whispered. "Mom. Come back."

Then I would get up and start pacing through the house again. I wondered when Maisie would get to Toronto. She had said she would go directly to the hospital.

After supper I stood in the living room, staring blankly out the window. Something blue moving outside caught my eye. It was Mrs. Silver, walking past our house, wearing a blue dress and a gray cardigan.

I went outside to speak to her. She looked at me kindly.

"Now how is your mother, Annie?" she asked.

"I don't know. She's had an operation, and we're waiting to see how she's doing."

Mrs. Silver reached over and gave my hand a squeeze. "She'll be fine, Annie. Is your grandmother coming?"

"Yes," I said. "But how did you—?"

She laughed. Her laugh sounded like a handful of tiny bells ringing. "Annie, I know all kinds of things. Don't you know who I am yet?"

"Umm . . . ummm . . . my fairy godmother?" I felt foolish saying it, but there was something fairylike about her and she did keep helping me.

Mrs. Silver laughed again. "Not exactly. I'm just someone who will never be far away and who will always be watching out for you. Even if you don't see me for a while, I'll always be there when you need me."

"Like a guardian angel?"

Mrs Silver smiled the sweetest smile and touched my cheek gently with her finger. It felt like the touch of a feather. "Yes, sort of like that. Now go back into the house. I think you're going to hear from the hospital soon."

I went back up the porch stairs, turning at the top to wave good-bye. She stood in the dappled light under the big chestnut tree and smiled, waving back.

Magda was at the door.

"Who were you waving at?" she asked.

"Mrs. Silver."

"Who?" Magda peered out into the street. "I don't see anyone."

"You know, Mrs. Silver. The old lady who lives down the street. She's standing right there under the tree."

Magda looked again, then shook her head and pulled me gently into the house.

"Are you okay, Annie? I saw you out there talking to yourself, and now you say there's someone there but . . ."

"She's right there," I said, turning and pointing. "She's walking away now."

Magda looked where I was pointing, right at Mrs. Silver, but she shook her head.

"I don't see anyone. Who is she?"

"Mrs. Silver? I see her nearly every day. She was there waiting with me at the library that time, when they called you to come get me. The day after the accident."

Magda stared at me. "There was no old lady with you that day. Just the librarian."

"But—"

"Never mind that now." Magda brushed my hair off my forehead and looked into my face, frowning. "It's been such a hard time for you, Annie." There were tears in her eyes. "We'll all be back to rights soon, don't you worry. Now, listen. Your dad just called and we need to go to the hospital."

My heart caught in my throat.

"Is Mom okay?"

"She's fine. She hasn't woken up yet but your dad thinks you should be there. He thinks it will help her."

Before we left, I ran up to the attic and pulled the red woolen blanket out of the trunk to take to Mom.

CLAIRE

I WAS COLD. I struggled up through a dream of long white corridors and breaking glass into my freezing bedroom, which was filled with the white light of the full moon. An icy Atlantic breeze found its way through the gaps in the window frame and slithered around my bed.

I jumped up, ran to the trunk in the corner and hauled out a red woolen blanket. As I turned to get back in bed, the moon pulled at me, and I wrapped the blanket around my shoulders and sat down in the big stuffed armchair. The glowing disc of the moon spilled light in a wide path across the water.

The beacon from the lighthouse flashed over the silver sea, a steady rhythm, every five seconds. Like a heartbeat. Like a drum.

"Annie," I whispered. "Where are you?"

"I'm right here, Mom."

I turned my head and there was Annie, smiling at me. "Wake up!" she said. "I've brought someone to see you."

"I am awake," I said.

Annie laughed. "Then open your eyes."

My head felt light and strange. I gave it a shake and the moon, and the ocean, and my bedroom at Crooked Head, all disappeared.

I was in a room with green curtains around my bed. A hospital? The red woolen blanket was still there, covering me. And

Annie was still there, smiling her head off. And behind her stood a tall woman with white curly hair and eyes the color of blueberries.

"Maisie?" I whispered.

She laughed and her eyes filled with tears. She came and took my hand.

"I've missed you," she said.

EPILOGUE

"Begin at the beginning," the King said, gravely, "and go on till you come to the end: then stop."

ALICE'S ADVENTURES IN WONDERLAND

ANNIE

I T WAS ONE of those hot days in late August when the sun beat down out of a brilliant blue sky. There was very little wind, and the ocean stretched away to the horizon in three directions from the lighthouse at Crooked Head. Maisie had brought some blankets out and laid them on the grass, and we'd had a picnic. Lemonade, tuna fish sandwiches, potato chips, chocolate cake. We all ate until we were stuffed, then lay back and stared into the deep blue that went on and on above us.

Mom lay on one side of me. Maisie on the other. You could still see where they had shaved Mom's hair away from her head when they did the operation. The hair was growing back but it looked funny. She was self-conscious about it and wore a hat when we went out. But she didn't mind Maisie and me seeing it.

"Ron is going to love this," said Mom.

"If it lasts," said Maisie.

Mom laughed. "Don't remind me. Newfoundland weather."

"But he'll be here in two days," I said. "Won't it still be summer?"

"Don't count on it," said Maisie.

———

We'd been at Crooked Head for a week, and the sun had been shining every day. I started to wonder if Mom had exaggerated about the rainy summers, but Maisie assured me that this was unusual weather, even for August, and the rain and the fog and the cold would return.

Mom was a lot better but still a little shaky, and she had a lot of headaches. Sometimes she couldn't find her words, but mostly she was okay. Dad said that would go away in a few weeks. Dr. Minto said she should recover fully.

Dad was worried about her coming to Newfoundland, but Dr. Minto said it would do her good to get away completely. And Maisie promised to look after her. For some reason, Dad and Maisie got on really well, right from the beginning. When Maisie showed up at the hospital that night, the day after Mom's operation, Dad was completely flabbergasted. He kept shaking his head and saying, "I don't understand. I thought you were dead." I tried not to laugh, but it was pretty funny to see him so confused. He didn't seem like a doctor at all then, just my dad.

Maisie did laugh, and gave him a big hug. "Not dead," she said. "Very much alive."

Dad turned red, but then he laughed too. From then on they were the best of friends.

I wish I could have heard the conversation between Mom and Dad when she tried to explain why she told him her mother was dead all those years. If they'd had it at home, I could have hidden in the closet and listened, but it happened at the hospital. She took a long time to completely wake up, and they kept her there for a month till they were sure there weren't going to be any complications.

It was fun to watch her and Maisie. The first few days, Mom kept forgetting why she was there, and we had to keep explaining it over and over. She and Maisie kept looking at each other, with exactly the same suspicious expression on their faces. They didn't look a lot alike, except for expressions like that. And their eyes. But they gradually grew more comfortable with each other.

I think it was the third day when they talked about the accident. Mom had been able to sit up that day and eat her lunch, but then she got really tired and lay back down and started to drift away. Maisie and I got up to leave, but Mom pulled on her sleeve.

"Maisie," she whispered. "I have to tell you something."

"So tell me," said Maisie, sitting down again.

Mom kept tight hold of her sleeve. "It's about Annie," she said.

Maisie glanced at me.

Mom shook her head. "No, about Little Annie. I need to tell you."

I kept very still. Maisie looked steadily at her.

"I never told you. I couldn't. But it was my fault. The accident. I wasn't holding her hand," and then tears started rolling down Mom's cheeks.

Maisie swallowed and seemed to be struggling not to start crying herself. Mom just waited, watching her mother's face. Finally Maisie reached out and smoothed the hair back from Claire's forehead.

"I know," she said. "I've always known. I saw the whole thing happen from the window. I knew you weren't holding her hand, no matter what you told me afterwards."

"But, but—" said Mom. "Why didn't you say anything? All those years? If you knew it was my fault?"

Maisie lost her battle with the tears. "Because it wasn't your fault, Claire. It was mine. I shouldn't have sent you out with Annie that day, when you were so fed up with her. I should have stopped working and taken you swimming like I said I would. It was my fault she died, not yours."

"No," said Mom. "I should have held her hand."

"She would have run anyway," said Maisie. "Even if you had been holding her hand, you couldn't have stopped her. And I don't know if even I could have stopped her."

They both looked at each other, tears streaming down their faces.

"It was an accident," said Mom.

Maisie nodded. "All this time we've both been blaming ourselves, but who knows why it happened or whether we could have stopped it. It was an accident and we've wasted all these years. I don't want to waste any more."

"No," said Mom in a shaky voice. Maisie leaned over and put her arms around her. For a moment, watching Mom's face, it seemed that twelve-year-old Claire was there, hugging her mother, finally at peace.

———

Maisie stayed with us, on the daybed in Dad's study. Magda liked her. I would hear the two of them cackling away in the kitchen, laughing about some story or other. Maisie and I went through all the presents in the trunk, and she told me how she made the sweaters and mittens and socks thinking about me, and hoping that someday she would meet me. I showed her all my sketchbooks and she gave me some advice about drawing and we had some really good talks about painting. We even went to some galleries together.

Maisie left before Mom got out of the hospital, after getting Mom to promise that she would come to Crooked Head later that summer.

I was so excited to get there. It was more or less like it was in the dreams, except the trees were bigger and the house was more fixed up. Maisie had the whole house now, and the first floor was opened up, but she'd left both staircases in, and upstairs you still went through the long closet to get into the other side. The second day there, Mom took me and Maisie into the downstairs hall of the Mirror House and turned the fish on the staircase. The painting was still there, wrapped in a sheet. Mom unwrapped it and Maisie just stood staring at it. Little Annie grinned out at us. She was making cookies in a sunny kitchen with a china Scottie dog standing on the windowsill behind her. Maisie couldn't speak.

Mom said, "Sorry, Maisie. I'm so sorry." And then they hugged and everyone cried a little.

They still disagreed about a lot of things. They would have little fights, and Mom would roll her eyes and look at me when Maisie was going on about something. I'd laugh. It was okay.

———

Maisie yawned and stretched.

"I'm going to go in and do some work while there's still light," she said, getting up.

Mom and I kept lying on the blanket. The sun felt deliciously warm on my face.

"Do you believe in ghosts?" I said to Mom after a while.

She looked thoughtful. "I did when I was your age. Maybe not so much anymore. But when I lived at Crooked Head, there was a man who helped my mother out with the house. Ed. Ed told me lots of ghost stories. And I used to read a lot about ghosts. There was even a time when I was convinced my little sister's ghost came back. That awful time just before I left Crooked Head. I thought Annie was here with me. I was sure I saw her. And she spoke to me. There was a fire . . ." Her words trailed off. "I guess I do believe in ghosts. What about you? Why do you ask?"

"Oh, just wondering. I found some books about ghosts in your bookcase."

———

I was staying in Claire's old room. It was weird at first, sleeping in her old bed, where we'd giggled about haunting Maisie and devoured the oatmeal cookies and the hot chocolate. It was difficult to put everything together in time, and hard to accept that I would never see the twelve-year-old Claire again. I missed her.

But I caught glimpses of her, now and then. When Mom got irritated with Maisie, or when something struck her funny, or when she got distracted and a wistful expression would appear in her eyes, then it was as if the ghost of young Claire walked into the room for a moment. I would hold my breath, hoping she would stay. But she never did. Not for long. I found myself searching for ways to bring her back.

One thing that did it was when we read *The Secret Garden* together. Mom confided in me that she'd never finished it because it reminded her too much of the accident. I persuaded her to read it with me. She would come and lie with me in her old bed before I went to sleep and read a couple of chapters to me. As she read her voice got younger and younger, and if I closed my eyes, I could imagine that it was Claire there with me, reading about the dead garden coming to life.

I couldn't bring myself to tell her about the dreams. It didn't seem right. They had cast a magic spell that brought me closer to her than I ever thought I could be. I didn't want to break that spell.

———

Mom yawned and sat up. "I think I need another nap, Annie." She smiled down at me. "I've never slept so much in my life. Are you coming in?"

I shook my head. "Not yet. I just want to get a little more sun." She gave my arm a little squeeze.

"Okay. See you later."

After she left I lay there for a while, soaking in the warmth. It felt so good to be there. I never wanted to go back to Toronto, but school started in another week or so. Mom had promised we could come back for a longer visit next summer.

Somebody was laughing, down the hill. I sat up and looked

out over the blue, blue ocean. The sun dazzled my eyes, but I thought I saw someone climbing over the rocks.

I blinked. There was someone. A little girl, about four years old, with curly brown hair and a big smile. She came up to me and laughed again.

"Annie?" I said, blinking again.

She put her finger up to her lips to shush me. Her eyes danced with mischief.

"Take care of them," she said. "They need you." And then she turned and went skipping off behind the lighthouse, humming a funny little song.

THE END

ACKNOWLEDGEMENTS

The story that would become *The Painting* came to me as a gift one sad summer after my foster sister, Marjory Noganosh, died. I worked on the novel over the next few years, during which time my mother also died. Although none of the characters in the book are based on Marjory or my mother, their spirits and their struggles infused my writing.

The painting "Ferryland Lighthouse" by the late Newfoundland artist, Gerald L. Squires, was the inspiration for Annie's painting and for the cover. I kept his vivid Newfoundland landscapes in mind when I wrote about Maisie's work. All the Squires family (Gerry, Gail, Meranda and Esther) shared stories with me about their time living at the Ferryland lighthouse in the 1970s, and Esther and I spent many hours talking about her childhood there. Again, none of the characters in my book are even remotely based on the Squires, but Esther's love of Ferryland and some of her ghost stories wiggled their way into the book.

Maybe it takes a village to help an author create a book: for me I had the generous support of grants from The Canada Council, The Newfoundland and Labrador Arts Council and Access Copyright Foundation. Escape to Create, a generous artist's residency in Seaside, Florida, gave me a month's writing time in a warm climate in February. Heaven! Special thanks to Marsha Dowler, whose hard work, affection and friendship helped to make that month such a sweet time for me.

Sally Keefe-Cohen has been a steady support and source of clarification on my contracts. Laurie Coulter and Sean Cotter both helped with extensive edits of my first chapters, and Michael Winter, Tracey Vaughan and Leigh Borden gave me reference letters and encouragement in equal measure. Thank you Sue Crocker and Tom Whalen for help with some Newfoundland expressions, and Brian Marler for the idea to hide the paintings in a staircase. And thanks to Tom and Baccalieu Cottage for the fish swimming up the stairs, and Jon Hsy for the informative discussion about English PhDs. Thank you Trudy Ruf and Simon Cotter (and Michael, Alexander and Emilia) for sharing your home with me as I passed through Toronto. And thank you Pat Green and Margaret Gardonio for all your thoughtful advice about the story. And for opening up your house and hearts to me on my travels and always being there for me, no matter what. A very special thanks to the late Ruth Darby, who showed me true friendship and her own unique perspective on being a mother. Thanks to Barb Neis and Peter Armitage for letting me be the ghost at their house in St. John's on many occasions. And I am grateful to Robin Cleland, whose insights gave me a much-needed boost midway through the writing process. And to Anita Levin, Camilla Burgess and Ananda Shakti, who all helped me through some very rough times while I was writing this book.

Heartfelt thanks to my editor, Samantha Swenson, for her enthusiasm, her astute (but gentle!) suggestions and her sense of humor. Thanks to Tara Walker for her ongoing support, Peter Phillips for being so cheerful whenever I ask him to do something for me, and everyone else at Tundra and Penguin Random House Canada Young Readers for their professionalism and dedication to good books. And a very special thanks to artist Jensine Eckwall for her creepy cover design. Yikes!

And big hugs and thank yous to my most ardent supporters: my sister, Cate Cotter, my father, Graham Cotter, and my daughter, Zoe Cleland. Thank you all for reading through the different versions of the book with unwavering appreciation. Thank you Cate for celebrating with me. Thank you Graham for nurturing my creativity on so many levels and for so many years! And thank you Zoe for all your love and understanding, and for the lasting insight into twelve-year-old girls you gave me long ago.

And finally, thanks to all mothers and daughters who continue to struggle to love each other and themselves. And especially to my own mother, Evelyn Cotter, whose enthusiasm, courage, laughter and love of books lives on.

"Ferryland Lighthouse" by Gerald L. Squires

ALSO BY CHARIS COTTER

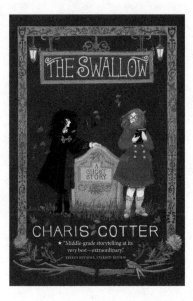

Polly and Rose have nothing in common . . . except ghosts. Polly wants to see one, Rose wishes she could stop seeing them. But is there more to Rose than it seems? Why does no one ever talk to her? And why does she look so . . . ghostly? When the girls find a tombstone with Rose's name on it in the cemetery and encounter an angry spirit in her house who seems intent on hurting Polly, they have to unravel the mystery of Rose and her strange family . . . before it's too late.

"Spooky tension, friendship and compassion permeate this exquisitely plotted middle-grade ghost story . . . Middle-grade storytelling at its very best—extraordinary."
– Starred Review, *Kirkus Reviews*

"Like all the best ghost stories, *The Swallow* tells us more about the living than the dead . . . all the makings of a classic."
– Starred Review, *Quill & Quire*

"An unusual ghost story with a revelation that readers will long remember."
– *Booklist*

"Halloween arrived early this year, with the release of Charis Cotter's ghost story *The Swallow*."
– *TIME for Kids*